Rick curled his fingers around hers, wondering if she could feel the increased tempo of his own heart.

"I should go help...help my mom," Becky whispered. But even as she spoke, she took a slow step closer.

"I think your mom can manage." Rick rubbed his thumb along the back of her hand, wondering what his next step was.

He didn't usually have to second-guess the next move. A hand under her chin. An encouraging smile. Then the kiss. All carefully choreographed and planned.

But he didn't want to treat her the same as he treated other women. She was special. He wanted to share more than a kiss. More than the physical expression of love. But she was a sincere Christian who loved her Lord. And he didn't know if he could share that with her.

Books by Carolyne Aarsen

Love Inspired

*Stealing Home

CAROLYNE AARSEN

has honed her writing between being a wife, stay-at-home mom, foster mom, columnist and business partner with her husband in their cattle and logging business in northern Alberta. Writing for Love Inspired is a blessed opportunity to combine her love for romance with her love for her Lord.

A HEART'S REFUGE

CAROLYNE AARSEN

Steeple
Hill®

Published by Steeple Hill Books™

STEEPLE HILL BOOKS

Steeple Hill®

ISBN 0-373-87278-X

A HEART'S REFUGE

Copyright © 2004 by Carolyne Aarsen

www.SteepleHill.com

Printed in U.S.A.

...his delight is in the law of the Lord.... He is like a tree planted by streams of water, which yields its fruit in season and whose leaf does not wither.

—*Psalms* 1:2 and 3

I want to dedicate this book to Dr. Randy Blacketer and Sandy Blacketer, our pastor and youth pastor. Two people who complement each other and our community in so many ways.
Thanks for your gifts of time and talents.

As well, I'd like to thank Laurie Carter from *Okanagan Life* and Karen Ball for their input on the magazine business.

Chapter One

Becky Ellison pressed her back against the outside door of *Going West*'s office, balancing her muffin, coffee cup and a batch of folders. Don't panic. You're just a little bit late.

"Hey, hon. Welcome back. How was the holiday?" Trixie sang out as Becky entered the reception area.

Becky set everything on the waist-high divider separating the entrance from Trixie Langston's domain and blew her breath out in a gusty sigh. "Breakfast on the run my first day back. Orders from our new boss that I'm deciphering late last night after spending ten days with hormonal teenage girls at Bible camp." She grabbed her hair in a ponytail and twisted an elastic around it. "You fill in the blanks."

"And such a lovely hairdo to impress our new boss." Trixie frowned as her eyes flicked over Becky's plaid shirt and blue jeans. Trixie, as usual, was immaculately groomed. Artfully windblown hairstyle. Pale pink sweater and gray skirt. Makeup. Earrings. Becky had never sought to emulate Trixie's style, but once in a while she wondered if people would take her more seriously if she did. "If this is your good impression," Trixie continued, "I would hate to see the slob version."

"Mom's wash machine broke down. The sewer backed up while Dad and Dennis were out in the orchard. After cleaning up that mess, this was all I had left to wear." Becky anchored a few loose strands behind her ear and bit her lips to make them red. "Okay, enough primping. I'll get my messages after the meeting. By the way, how late am I?"

Trixie glanced at the clock in the foyer of the magazine office. "I'd love to say everyone else is running their usual fifteen minutes behind, but for once everyone is early. Except you."

Becky pulled a face at Trixie, stifling the dread that clutched her midsection. Rick Ethier. Here in Okotoks. What were the odds that he remembered who she was? Probably slim to none. She probably knew more about him than he did about her. She sucked in another breath. "My friend, wish me luck."

"Give him your best smile and you'll do fine," Trixie said, flashing her a thumbs-up.

The door of Nelson's office was shut and the only sound she heard was an unfamiliar deep voice. Rick, most likely. New publisher of the magazine her father started and Rick's grandfather, Colson Ethier, recently purchased.

Up until three weeks ago, office gossip was Nelson, the previous publisher, would stay on after the purchase. Then, just before she left on her so-called holiday— camp counselor to ten teenage girls—she was stunned to discover that Rick Ethier, Colson Ethier's grandson, would take over Nelson's job. Now she would be making an entrance, and a poor first impression, in front of the man who had shattered so many of her hopes and dreams.

She smoothed one hand over her still damp hair, drew in a slow breath, sent up a quick prayer and carefully opened the door. Flashing everyone an apologetic smile, she dropped into her usual chair beside Nelson's desk, uncomfortably close to her new boss. She dropped her papers on the corner of Nelson's desk and chanced a look at Rick Ethier standing beside her.

His face was all too familiar, though the grainy magazine picture indelibly imprinted on her mind didn't capture the reality of his good looks in person. Shaggy blond hair framed the kind of face that would make women of any age stop and take a second look. The hint of a dimple in his cheek balanced out the self-assured cockiness of his smile, and his eyes were so intensely blue it was as if they glimmered with an interior light. His clothing was a mixture of casual and stylish. He wore a soft cotton cream-colored shirt, a deep brown corduroy blazer and fitted blue jeans.

And as he glanced Becky's way, a frown.

Please don't let him state the obvious, she thought, carefully setting her coffee cup on the floor beside her.

Instead he glanced at his watch. Almost as bad.

"Sorry I'm late," she said with a quick smile as she reached over and shook his hand. "I'm Becky Ellison."

"Our editor," Rick said, returning her smile with a cool one of his own. "Glad you could make it." He held her gaze a moment, as if establishing his territory, then he turned to face the rest of the gathered staff of the magazine, dismissing her. "As you all now know, I'm Rick Ethier, grandson of Colson Ethier, the new owner of *Going West*. I'm sure you're wondering why my grandfather, whose holdings are fairly substantial, would bother himself with one small, regional magazine. Trust me, I'm as baffled."

A few titters greeted that comment, but Becky heard the faint cynicism in his remark. A trademark of his.

Rick Ethier was a travel writer for Colson Ethier's flagship magazine. Though he couldn't be more than thirty, his stories and articles usually held a shadow of world-weariness. As if he'd seen it all. Done it all.

And as Becky listened to him, one part of her mind easily resurrected other words of one particularly scathing article. "Sentimental claptrap" and "shamelessly manipulative." These less than flattering descriptions came from a monthly book review column Rick wrote for the same magazine. A column in which Rick wrote about the first book Becky had published. Her pride and joy. And thanks to that negative review, Becky hadn't been able to get a second contract with her publisher.

Focus on the now, Becky, she reminded herself, taking a long slow breath to ease away her irritable emotions. This was her new boss, and no matter what, she had to learn to get along with him. The past was past.

"I've done my research on this magazine," Rick was saying, "but for now, I want to go around the room and ask each of you what you see as the purpose of *Going West*. The vision, so to speak."

Feet shuffled, a few throats cleared as the staff glanced around the room at each other. Becky sat back in her chair, crossing her feet at the ankles, surprised at the momentary blankness in her own mind.

Going West was supposed to have a vision?

Nelson, the previous publisher and her father's partner, had set the tone and layout of the magazine from its inception. He had reviewed, accepted and or rejected freelance articles. Since Becky started working as editor, she had simply followed his lead, hoping she caught the idea of what he wanted for that particular issue.

Never had they sat down and reviewed—or even spoke of—any kind of long-term vision.

"Why don't we start with you, Becky, now that you've deigned to join us." Rick stood beside his presentation board, his arms crossed, his legs apart, his head tilted to one side.

Definitely hostile body language, thought Becky with a surge of anger. She shouldn't have been late. But that was also past.

"We can do that." Becky licked her lips, buying time as hazy, insubstantial thoughts slipped past her defensive emotions. C'mon, Becky. Think. This is your chance to show Rick Ethier that you are intelligent and articulate. Not sentimental in the least.

"I've always seen *Going West* as firstly a regional magazine," she said, grasping at an idea that she knew to be true. "Our second mandate is to be a magazine disseminating a viewpoint peculiar to Western sensibilities."

Rick nodded, his lips pursed. "Can we try that in English?"

Becky held his direct gaze, trying not to be unnerved by his glinting eyes. In spite of her resolve to forget, snatches of his nasty book review sifted through her head. "Verbose, treacly and unrealistic."

"It's a cowboy and farmer magazine," she snapped.

"That's probably closer to the mark," Rick said with a humorless half grin.

Becky held his gaze a moment, as if challenging him, but she was the first to look away.

The meeting went downhill from there. People who had received minimal guidance from Nelson or, to be honest, her father, now had to come up with a thumbnail sketch of what the magazine was supposed to accomplish.

Advertising. Art. Circulation. While they struggled through their answers, Becky felt embarrassed and exposed.

They should all know, she thought, taking a pencil out from behind her ear. But Nelson's editorial meetings tended to be haphazard. He and Becky sat down once a week going over articles and their status, laying out the magazine's plan for that particular month. When they wrote up the schedule for the upcoming magazines, there was an underlying cohesion, but a person had to go looking to find it.

But vision? Simply not there.

She scribbled a few things down on paper, took a few notes from what people were saying.

"So you can see—" Rick flipped over the first page of the presentation chart "—all this vagueness has translated into this." He pointed to a listing of numbers he had written down.

"Circulation is down, subscription is down. Advertising revenue is down. And I'm going to attribute all that to what I'm hearing in this room this morning."

Rick looked around, letting his direct gaze tick over each of them, then finally coming back to Becky. "Which is a lot of vague words, but no single, clear statement that outlines what this magazine is really about. And that is going to change. As of today."

He had done his homework, Becky thought with grudging respect.

"So what's your first step?" Becky asked. Rick's language made it very clear that he was lead dog. She just needed to know where he was heading.

"Sitting down with my editor and laying out my vision for this magazine."

A cold finger of apprehension snaked down her back. "Your vision?"

Rick shrugged, rocking lightly back on his heels. "Media is all about communication. I haven't heard much in this room, other than your cowboy and farmer comment, that creates a concise and clear idea of what *Going West* is supposed to be."

He didn't know the community. The surrounding area. How was he going to come up with the direction of the magazine? And where did *he* see it going?

"Branding is the name of the game in publishing," Rick continued. "Now I need to figure out what brand of magazine we are going to become."

His words were not comforting.

"I've already commissioned a marketing analysis team to do surveys, interview focus groups and send out questionnaires to our current readership. That won't be coming in for a couple of months, but that doesn't mean we can't make some changes now." He perched on the edge of Nelson's desk and glanced around the room.

"I'm going to be sitting down with each member of the various departments and going over what we've got coming up and what we can possibly change for now."

Becky rubbed the back of her neck. Rick's plans translated into work she didn't have time for. She had a long-term commitment to the youth choir at church. She had promised the school librarian she'd help weed through books that needed to be sold or discarded. A fund-raising committee had asked her to write copy for their brochure.

She had Bible study. Book club.

And somehow in the middle of all this she needed to put together a stellar proposal that would negate any second thoughts her publisher had about working with her.

"I hope this isn't going to be a problem, Miss Ellison?"

Becky looked up. Had her disappointment shown on her face?

Rick faced her, his eyebrows raised, his eyes boring into hers. "You seem disheartened."

It *had* shown.

Becky glanced around the room. She wasn't the only disheartened one, but somehow Rick had zeroed in on her.

She stifled her resentment and chose her words carefully. "I'm just thinking about all the work ahead for each department. It's going to be difficult to turn the direction of this magazine around midstream."

Rick flipped his hand to one side, as if dismissing her concerns. "Any change we implement is going to take some sacrifice and time." He gestured toward the chart behind him. "The figures speak for themselves. If this magazine keeps going in the direction it is, most of the people in this room are going to be out of a job. The only choices available to you now are hard work." Rick looked around the room, his arms crossed, his legs spraddled in a defensive posture. "Or no work."

There was nothing more to be said. Rick waited a heartbeat more. "Meeting's over," he said. "You're dismissed."

Cliff Thiessen let his chair drop back onto the floor with a thud and got up. "Well, better get back to it," he muttered to no one in particular. As the rest of the staff left, there was some muttering, but for the most part people were subdued by what their new boss had told them.

"Becky, I'd like to see you a moment," Rick said as she gathered up her papers in preparation for leaving.

Panic tightened her chest, but she masked it with a vague smile. She thought she had done pretty good up till now. She didn't know if she could handle a face-to-face meeting quite yet.

She shuffled through her papers while the room emptied, buying some time.

"What can I do for you?" she said, once the door closed behind the last person.

"I just wanted to take a moment to speak with you privately." Rick walked around to the other side of Nelson's desk, glancing out the bank of windows that filled one wall. Becky couldn't help follow the direction of his gaze. Beyond the roofs of Okotoks, the golden prairie rolled toward the soft brown of the Porcupine Hills, which nudged against the jagged peaks of the Rocky Mountains, faintly purple in the morning sun.

"It's a beautiful view, isn't it?" she said quietly.

"It will help compensate for having to live out here for a while."

Cynicism again. She shouldn't have been surprised. "What do you mean?"

Rick turned back to her and rested his hands palms down on his desk. "You may as well know, I'm here a maximum of twelve months and that's it. My grandfather issued me an ultimatum I have a lot of incentive to keep."

Becky frowned lightly, but held his steady gaze. "What ultimatum?"

"Turn this magazine around in twelve months and he'll leave me alone to go back to traveling and living my life as I see fit."

"And then what happens to the magazine?"

Rick shrugged and pushed himself off from the desk. "Not my concern."

"Will your grandfather still own it?"

"I don't know. You could buy it if you wanted." His casual words held a lash of mockery.

"I've got my own plans," she said softly.

"And what would those be?"

Try to ease away from the relentless deadlines of magazine work. Write a book that would make her current editor sit up and take notice. Offer her the temporary stability of a multibook contract.

But Rick Ethier was the last person she was going to dump her "treacly" dreams on.

"I've got a few things on the go." She drew in a slow breath and looked up at him again. He was watching her, his head canted to one side, his mouth softer now that it no longer was twisted into a cynical smile.

And in spite of her negative feelings toward him, she

felt a nebulous connection spark between them, then lengthen into a gentle warmth.

She was the first to look away, confusion fighting her initial antagonism. What was wrong with her? So he was good-looking. So he possessed a certain charm that it seemed even she wasn't immune to.

He was her boss. And the man who had a hand in delaying her dream.

Rick cleared his throat and shuffled some file folders on his desk. "I understand from Nelson that you have been working on setting up an appointment with the Premier of Alberta?"

"I don't have a firm commitment, but I'm in communication with his secretary."

"Congratulations. That's quite a coup. I've been trying to get an interview with him since he was voted in with such an overwhelming majority."

"Jake's pretty private."

"I'll say. He guards his private life like a Doberman. I've tried a few times to get an interview for Colson's magazine, but I've always been turned away with a polite but firm no."

Becky knew this about Jake. In fact, he had said the only reason he would consider an interview with her was because he knew it wouldn't turn into a gossipfest. Before he had become premier of Alberta and after, she and Jake Groot had been members of a province-wide committee devoted to preservation of native grasslands. They had gotten to know each other on a social as well as committee level and Becky had used that leverage to snag this formal interview.

"I'd like to help you with that article."

The cold finger she had felt before became an icy fist. "Actually, I always work on my own," she said quietly but firmly.

"When is the interview?" he asked, ignoring her comment.

"Not for a few months."

"Keep me in the loop, then."

He's your boss, Becky reminded herself when she looked up at him. "Okay, I'll do that," she said quietly. More than that she wasn't going to promise. Jake would not be pleased if she dragged along a whole phalanx of people.

She gathered up her papers and Rick laid his hand on hers. She flinched as if she'd been burned.

"Sorry, I believe that's mine." He pointed to the small burgundy engagement calendar in her hands.

"I don't think so," Becky said, shifting the papers that were threatening to spill out of her arms. "It has my initials on it. *R.E.*"

Rick held up a similar calendar and frowned down at it. "This one has the same initials."

Becky flipped hers open to a page with a butterfly sticker in one corner and a reminder to pick up butter scribbled in purple pen on a stained and dog-eared page.

"This is mine," she muttered, closing it and slipping it between her papers and her chest.

"I'm sorry," Rick said, tapping the folder he held against his other hand. "I'm guessing Becky is short for Rebecca."

Good-looking *and* smart, Becky thought with a touch of her own cynicism. "You've got that right," she said, flashing him a quick smile.

And as she left his office, she blew out a sigh. One day down. Only three hundred and sixty four to go.

"You knew Rick Ethier was going to be taking over from Nelson, so why are you so angry?" Sam Ellison asked, crouching down beside another sapling.

"I guess the reality was harder than the idea." Becky dug her hands into the sun-warmed dirt of the new apple orchard. An early-evening breeze fanned away the warmth of the sun, and she could already feel the peace of the orchard easing away the tension of the day. "I mean I just found out before I went to camp. That hardly gave me time to get used to the idea."

"You'll get used to it. Hand me the budding knife please."

She pulled the small, but deadly sharp blade out of the toolbox her father carried with him and watched while he painstakingly cut a T shape in the bark of the young sapling. "I got the impression from Colson that he's quite proud of his grandson," Sam continued. "Rick's travel articles are quite insightful."

"As are his nasty book reviews." Becky couldn't keep the disdainful tone out of her voice, netting her a light frown from her father. "I still don't understand why such a prestigious magazine chose my book to review."

"That was a year ago, Becky."

"And since then, the publisher has been pretty hesitant about buying another book."

"Your editor is behind you."

"He's been great, but if he can't sell it to the marketing people who seem to have a copy of that nasty review branded on their brain tissues, I'm just spinning my wheels." She leaned forward, yanking an isolated stalk of grass from the newly cultivated dirt. "I don't know if Rick even realized it's my book he slammed—a casualty of his cutting words. I'm left bleeding on the sidelines while he moves on, blithely unaware of what he had done." With a dramatic flourish she raised her face to the sky and pressed her hand to her chest.

"When you're finished declaiming, you can hand me that whip please. The Alberta Red."

"See, not even my own father appreciates my pain." With a grin Becky plucked a tree branch out of the bucket of water. She carefully sliced the bud off it herself, taking a large piece of bark with it. Turning it over she plucked the pith away from the backside of the slice and handed it to her father.

"Change isn't always a bad thing, Becky. Life is always about adapting." He inserted the slice in the cut, against the live flesh of the sapling, pulled the bark back over top and secured it with a rubber band. "Rick can bring in a new way of looking at things."

"He talks about finding a new direction for the magazine, but how can he when he doesn't know the community it targets?"

"That can be good. He'll bring his own perspective and skills to the magazine. Like bringing new genetic material into the orchard and grafting it onto established and mature stock."

"Except he's only here for a while, which makes me wonder if the 'graft' will take. He's a wanderer, just like Trevor was."

"Don't tell me you're still mooning over him?" Sam held out his hand. "Can I have that pine tar please?"

Becky handed him a small tin and a flat stick. "Hardly mooning. Trevor was a high school romance and a reminder to stay away from guys who can't commit." She curled her legs closer to herself and hugged them. "Anyway, Rick said he's only going to be around a year. Maybe less. That's hardly long enough to make a real difference. I'm sure he wants to go back to his traveling. Last I heard it was Malta. Before that Thailand."

Sam wrapped protective covering over the wound and gave Becky an indulgent smile. "Seems to me you know a fair bit of what is going on in Rick Ethier's life."

Becky avoided his eyes. She could try to make some lame excuse about her knowledge of Rick's comings and goings but she had never been a very good liar.

"How in the world did you and Colson even connect?" Becky asked, handing her father his toolbox as he pushed himself to his feet.

"Years ago, Colson lived in Calgary and had courted your grandmother. He decided the real money was back East, but she wouldn't leave Okotoks." Sam gave Becky a hand up. "Maybe he is taking a short trip down memory lane, buying this magazine."

"And taking a very reluctant passenger with him. Rick."

"Well, you make sure to invite him out here sometime."

Becky sighed as she slipped her arm through her father's. "Give me some time to get used to the idea that he's even here in Okotoks. In my office."

The heat emanating from the dark plowed ground gave way to a soft coolness as they entered the older orchard.

"I'm going to have to get rid of some of these trees," her father mused, looking up at the gnarled branches. "Though I hate to."

"'Every tree that does not bear fruit must be cut down and cast into the fire,'" Becky quoted, giving her father's arm a jiggle as if to remind him.

"God gives us lots of chances. I think I might let these trees go another year or two." He reached up and touched one branch, the dearth of apples on it a silent testimony to their uselessness. "I can still take a few cuttings from them."

"You say that every year, Dad," Becky said with a smile.

Becky's maternal great-grandfather started this orchard when he first immigrated from Holland. It was a gamble to expect to create an oasis on the harshly bald prairie. But the soil proved fertile and the poplar trees planted as windbreaks shot up, creating a refuge necessary for the apple trees to flourish. Irrigation came from a creek that flowed through the property.

The orchard had gone through three generations and various changes. Becky's mother, Cora, inherited the orchard. When Cora Bruinsma married Sam Ellison, he slowly worked his way into the family business, helping to cultivate the orchard and keeping the magazine going at the same time.

Becky grew up with her time split between the hustle and bustle of the magazine and the peace of the orchard. Her first love was writing, but her home was her sanctuary. Her plan had been to stay at home until she had her second book published and a contract for another. Only then would she feel she had the financial wherewithal to buy a place of her own and move out.

Which hadn't happened yet.

And if she didn't get working on this next book, wasn't likely to happen for at least another year.

* * *

"*Going West.* Becky speaking." Becky tucked the phone under her ear, she pushed the sleeves of her sweater up and drew the copy of the article she had been working on toward her. Sneaking a quick glance at her watch—2:15 p.m. She had fifteen minutes yet.

"Becky? This is Gladys Hemple. I do the cooking and preserves column."

"What can I do for you, Gladys?" Becky's pencil flicked over the paper, striking out, putting in question marks.

Gladys didn't reply right away. Becky heard a faint sniff, then...

"You know I get a lot of compliments on the column," Gladys said, her voice suspiciously thick. "Lots of people say they read it all the time."

"So what's the problem?" Becky frowned when she heard another, louder sniff over the phone.

"I've been asked not to do it anymore." Another sniff. "By some man named Rick who says he's the new publisher."

Becky laid her pencil down, her full attention now on her caller. "What exactly did he say, Gladys?"

"That he's changing the focus of the magazine and that what I do didn't mesh with the vision. Or something like that." Gladys paused and Becky heard her blowing her nose. "Becky, I've been doing that column for the past twenty-five years and I was never late. Not even once. What did I do wrong?"

Becky clutched the phone in her hand and leaned back in her chair. "Gladys, I'm sure there's been some mistake. I'll go talk to Mr. Ethier."

"Could you do that please? I've just finished taking pictures of the chocolate cake for this week's recipe. I hate to see it all wasted."

"You just get those pictures developed. I'll deal with Rick."

And bring that cake over here.

Becky stomach growled at the thought of Gladys Hemple's chocolate cake. She hadn't eaten or taken a break since she'd grabbed a couple of bites out of the stale muffin she'd found while scavenging through her desk for a pen that worked. That had been eight-thirty.

In fifteen minutes she had a meeting with Rick and she still had a couple of articles to go over. Becky had re-edited half of the articles already slated for the next issue to nudge them in the direction Rick wanted to take this magazine. The extra workload had meant she'd missed her bible study and had to cancel another library board meeting.

The phone rang again.

Becky stifled her resentment and put a smile on her face. "*Going West.* Becky speaking."

"This is Alanna Thompson."

Becky closed her eyes, massaging the bridge of her nose with her fingers, and sent up a prayer for patience and peace. Alanna wasn't known for her reticence. And noting the restrained fury in Alanna's voice, Becky was pretty sure she knew the reason she was calling.

"How can I help you, Alanna?"

"What in the world is going on there? I just got a phone call from some guy named Rick Ethier. He just told me he's returning the four articles that the magazine bought. Who is this guy?"

Becky blew out her breath, suddenly aware of the tension in her shoulders. Which columns to cut and which articles to send back should have been her call. Not Rick's. At least he could have waited until their meeting this afternoon to consult with her.

"Rick is our new publisher."

"What does that have to do with anything?"

"With a new publisher comes a new direction," Becky offered, struggling not to let her own anger seep into her voice. "Rick obviously has a different idea of how he sees *Going West* than Nelson did."

And from the sounds of things Rick's vision didn't include baking or horses, cowboys and farmers.

"You know how much time I spent on those? How many horse trainers I interviewed? All the pictures I took? And not on spec. You told me the magazine would buy them all." Alanna's fury grew with each sentence she threw at Becky. "I got some great material together."

"You'll be released to submit them elsewhere," Becky said, her frustration growing. "And of course there's our kill fee."

"There had better be."

"Look, I'm sorry." A faint nagging pain started at one temple, threatening to take over her whole head. Alanna's yelling only intensified her frustration with Rick. And her headache. If she didn't get something to eat pretty soon, she was sure it was going to become a full-blown migraine. "I'm sorry about this, Alanna," Becky said, trying to keep her voice quiet. Soothing. "You've done great work for us in the past and I appreciate all the hard work you've put into all your articles. Good luck selling the articles somewhere else."

The harsh click in her ear told Becky how soothing her words had been.

Becky shoved her hands through her hair and grabbed the back of her neck. It felt as tight as a guitar string.

And in five minutes she had to face Rick Ethier.

She wondered if she had time to run across the street and grab a bite to eat. Better not. Instead she pulled open her desk drawer and pulled out the grease-stained bag. She shook out the rest of the muffin into her hand and popped it into her mouth. Two days old, but it was a much-needed snack.

She gathered up her papers and slipped them all into her portfolio, along with her Day-Timer. A paper covered with scribbles fluttered to the floor and she bent to pick it up. Notes for her most recent book.

Since Rick had come, she hadn't had a spare minute to work on it. And if the past few days were any indication of the work Rick required to change the magazine's direction, she wouldn't have any time until Rick left.

In twelve months.

Dear Lord, am I ever going to get anywhere with my writing? The prayer was a cry of despair. She looked over at her crowded bookshelf. Her own book sat tucked away amongst all the others. But one book does not a career make, and if she wanted to live her dream, she needed at the least a multibook contract.

All her life she had wanted to be a fiction writer. But she had loans to repay and she had to live. So she took the job her father offered and for three years she had poured her heart and soul into that first book in her infrequent spare time.

When she received the call that this, her first book, had been bought, she broke down and cried like a baby. Then she celebrated.

Though her parents were overjoyed for her, her mother had given her the best advice. Advice, she was sure, countless other authors had received.

"Don't quit your day job."

So she stayed on with *Going West,* editing and writing nonfiction during the day, writing fiction in the evening, begrudging each minute away from her work as she put together her next book.

Then came Rick's review, the sales figures just behind that, and her publisher started stalling on a contract for her option book. And now she didn't have the time to work on it.

Becky pushed herself away from her desk. Enough wallowing. She had other things to discuss with Rick.

Such as maintaining her "day job."

Chapter Two

Becky strode down the hallway to Rick's office but was stopped when she faced the closed door. One of the many changes that had swept through this office since Rick took over. She knocked lightly.

"Come in."

To her surprise, Rick wasn't elbow-deep in the computer printouts that dominated his desk, but instead stood by the window, looking out over the town to the mountains beyond.

"I love the view from this office," Becky said with forced cheer. She was going to be nice. Going to be a good example of Christian love. "Though it always makes me want to quit what I'm doing and head out to the mountains."

Rick shrugged. "I suppose it could, if you were the impulsive type."

In spite of her good intentions Becky felt her back bristle.

Nice. Nice. I'm going to be nice.

"So what did you want to discuss today?" she asked,

sitting in her usual chair in one corner of Nelson's office.

She wanted to give him a chance to talk before she brought up her own grievances.

"I've been working on clearing up the deadwood." Rick dropped into his chair, massaging his temple with his forefinger. "This magazine is practically in the Dark Ages."

"Considering that we don't use a Gutenberg press to put out the paper, that seems a bit extreme," Becky said, tempering her comment with a smile.

Rick gave her a level glance but Becky held her ground. She had promised to be nice, but he didn't need to be so cutting.

"Just because *Going West* has a glossy cover doesn't mean it's keeping up." Rick pushed himself ahead, pulling a pencil out of the holder on a now-tidy desk. "We've got to move forward."

"From the phone calls I've been getting, that means leaving behind people like Gladys Hemple and Alanna Thompson."

Rick shrugged again. "Alanna was a terrible writer. Overly emotional and bombastic. Gladys, an anachronism."

"I would think that would be my call to make." Her words came out clipped. Tight.

"Would you have cut them?"

Becky held his gaze, trying to distance himself from the harshness of Rick's words, so close to what he had said about her own writing.

"I don't know. I guess it would have depended on this 'vision' we are going to talk about right now."

"They don't fit. I would have told you to cut them anyhow."

Becky held his gaze, realizing that she was dealing with a far different sort of publisher than Nelson and his easygoing approach.

"And who or what are we going to replace them with?"

"I've got a guy lined up to do a weekly column. Gavin Stoddard."

Becky struggled to keep smiling. To stay positive as her brain scrambled for words that weren't confrontational. "Gavin has a rather cynical take on Okotoks. What would he do a column on?"

"He's on the local chamber of commerce. He has a thriving business in an area that's expanding. He's exactly the kind of person that can give some helpful advice to other businesses."

"So that's your focus? Business?"

Rick leaned forward. "In order to increase advertising revenue, we have to make the magazine appealing to the business sector of our readership."

"But more ads means fewer features. That would make it..." She stopped just short of saying "boring." Too confrontational.

"Make it what?"

She waved the comment aside. "I would like to get back to Alanna and Gladys. Please let me know before you do something like that again, so we can discuss this together." She held her ground, knowing that she was right. "It makes my job difficult otherwise. I'm still editor and I prefer that we work together."

Rick swayed in his chair, his finely shaped mouth

curved into a humorless smile. "Do you think that can happen?" he asked.

Becky accepted the challenge in his gaze even as she thought of the book she couldn't finish. She needed this job for now, but she wasn't going to get pushed around.

"I think it can. As long as we keep talking."

But even as she spoke the words, Becky realized he had been right about one thing that he had said earlier.

Twelve months was going to be far too long.

The day had disappeared, Rick thought, looking up at the darkening sky with a flash of regret.

This morning, when he came to the office, the sun was a shimmer of light in the east, the dark diminishing in the west. Now the bright orange globe hovered over the western horizon. In the east, the dark was now gaining.

While he was tied to his desk, dealing with reluctant employees, courting new advertisers, wrestling with his editor over the new plan for this magazine, the sun had stolen across the sky and he had lost an entire day.

Glowering, he walked to his vehicle, a battered and rusty Jeep. He patted its dented hood, as if commiserating with it. "Only eleven months and twenty days to go," he murmured, "and we can be on the road again. *Outside* during the day, the way we should be." He glanced around once more. The town looked complacent this time of evening. Most people were, he was sure, sitting at the dinner table, eating with their families.

Domestic bliss.

An oxymoron as far as he was concerned. When he and his mother lived with Colson, all he remembered of domesticity were large cold rooms that echoed as he walked to the wing of the house that his grandfather had set aside for Rick and his mother. He remembered sad music and the sounds of his mother's muffled crying.

When she died, Rick's life became a round of boarding schools during the year, and nannies and housekeepers over the summer months.

Colson remained a shadowy figure in Rick's life. A figure to whom Rick spent most of his youth trying to gain access. And trying to please.

Rick did a monthly book review column for his grandfather's magazine, one of Colson's many enterprises, as a way of acknowledging Colson's contribution to his education. Through it he enjoyed the chance to take a contrary view of some of the more popular literary works lauded by other critics.

But it was traveling that ignited a passion in him he didn't feel for anyone or anything else. It provided a ready-made conduit for his articles, and the money they made him became a way to finance more trips. He usually found time to make semiannual duty trips back to Toronto to connect with his editor and, of course, to see his grandfather.

Going home always turned to be a straightforward debriefing of what he had done, how he was doing. But in the past year Colson had been getting more involved in Rick's life—putting increased pressure on him to join the family enterprise, inviting him to supper, with eligible young women in attendance.

This put Rick in a quandary. He felt he owed his grandfather, but at the same time didn't think he had to mold his entire life around Colson's whims. It came to an ugly head in a confrontation, which led Colson to offer Rick this ultimatum. Bring this small-town magazine Colson had bought on a whim to profitability in twelve months and Colson would leave him alone for the rest of his life. That was all Colson required of him and Rick had reluctantly accepted. It was only the thought that he wouldn't have to listen to Colson's tired lectures on Christian faith and Rick's lack of it that made Rick accept this position.

Rick stopped at one of the few streetlights in town and glanced over at the café, the lights and the bustle within luring him on. He was hungry but didn't feel like eating alone in the furnished apartment he had rented. At least at Coffee's On, the crowd would provide some semblance of company.

The café was surprisingly full, this time of evening. Rick paused in the doorway, letting the clink of cutlery, the chatter of conversation wash over him. He nodded at the owner of a car dealership he had met yesterday on his trip with the sales team around town, smiled at one of the waitresses who hustled past him.

He glanced around the café looking for an empty table. As he walked farther inside he spotted one beside Becky Ellison.

Becky sat at her table, chin in hand, staring out the window, her laptop open in front of her. The overhead light caught flashes of red in her auburn hair, burnished her skin glowing peach.

When she had bustled into the meeting room, that first morning, late, laden with papers, coffee and a muffin, he couldn't help feel a frisson of energy and attraction. There was something beguiling about her that drew his eyes, his attention to her. He didn't want to be as firm with her as he had, but the magazine staff had been working together for some time, making him the interloper.

Something that was made fairly clear to him the first time he and his editor spoke.

Antagonism radiated from her from the moment she raised her hazel eyes to his. And in most of the meetings since then the feeling only seemed to grow.

But tonight there were no other empty places, so with some resignation Rick walked over to the table beside hers and sat down.

Becky's gaze was averted so she didn't see him. She wore her hair down today instead of pulled back in her usual clip. A half smile played over her lips as she absently toyed with her hair.

If it wasn't for the fact that Rick knew Becky didn't care much for him, he'd be more attracted than he was.

"Coffee?" The waitress came between his table and Becky's and he looked up.

"No. Just a glass of water. And you can bring me the special."

Her wide smile gave Rick's ego a light boost.

The sound had broken Becky's reverie. As if waking from a dream, she blinked, straightened up, then looked around.

Rick could tell the instant she saw him. Once again the smile faded and once again he was treated to a detachment that negated the little lift he'd gotten just seconds ago.

"Hey, there," he said, leaning back in his chair. He folded his arms across his chest, a defensive gesture, he had to admit. "Taking work home?"

Becky glanced at her computer and gently closed

the top, a surprising flush coloring her cheeks. She looked as if he had caught her doing something illegal. "No. Just a writing project I've been spending my scant spare time on." Her tone was careful, almost resentful.

Writing project. Obviously not work, or she would have said so. Formless thoughts tumbled through his head.

"What kind of writing project?" he asked, intrigued in spite of himself.

"A book."

"That takes a lot of time."

"Exactly. Trouble is, I can't seem to find the time."

Rick grinned. "One thing I learned is that you don't find time to write. You make time and then defend it. You'll never get a book written by 'finding' time."

"I have written one book already," Becky said, her voice taking on a defensive note.

"Really? What kind?"

She lifted her chin in a defensive gesture. "Fiction."

Rick could only look at her as his thoughts coalesced. Becky. *Rebecca.* "You wrote a book called *Echoes.*"

She nodded.

"I did a review of one of your books, didn't I? For my grandfather's magazine?"

Becky's only response was to look away, but he knew he was right. He remembered now.

"I gather the review wasn't favorable." He couldn't remember the details of what he had written. The editor of his grandfather's magazine liked Rick's reviews because he wasn't afraid to go against the grain and pronounce a currently popular literary novel prose without purpose.

Obviously he had done just that with Becky's book.

"'Wasn't favorable'?" she repeated, fixing him with a steady gaze. "Try unnecessarily cutting. Or sarcastic." She looked like she was about to say something more, but she pressed her lips together.

Rick let her words wash over him as he had done with other authors and authors' fans. He refused to take her seriously, his opinion was his own opinion, and as he tried to explain again and again, it was one opinion. If writers couldn't take criticism, they had better try something else.

"So it's not because I'm some Eastern interloper that you tend to be slightly ticked off at me."

Becky angled her head to one side, as if studying him. "That, too."

Rick leaned forward and cocked her a wry grin. "Get used to it, sweetie. I'm around for a while."

She held his gaze, her eyes steady. "Don't call me 'sweetie,'" she said quietly. "It's insincere."

Was it?

Maybe she wasn't a "sweetie," per se—her tawny eyes and crooked grin negated that image—but there was definitely something about her that appealed. In spite of her off-putting attitude. "Maybe I'm teasing," he said.

"Maybe you should be nice."

"You could teach me." The comment sounded lame, but he couldn't think of anything snappier to say.

"Well, you know the saying, if you can't say something nice, become a reporter."

He couldn't stop his burst of laughter. "You are in the right job."

The waitress came just then with his order. "Here you go. I hope you enjoy." She gave him a broad smile, lingered just long enough to show her interest but not long enough to create an embarrassing situation, and was gone. But she didn't hold his interest.

The woman who did was packing up, and to his surprise, Rick felt a twinge of disappointment. It had been a while since he'd spent any time with a pretty woman. An even longer time with one who didn't seem to be afraid to challenge him.

"The muse desert you?" he asked, unwrapping his utensils.

"She's been a bit flighty lately." Becky slipped her laptop into a knapsack.

"You're so fond of mottoes, surely you know that for writers, when the going gets tough..." Rick let the sentence trail off.

"The tough writers huddle under their desk chewing the cuffs of their sleeves," Becky finished off for him.

He couldn't help it. He laughed again.

She slipped her knapsack over her shoulder and pulled her hair loose from the straps, shooting him an oblique smile as she did so. With a muttered "See you tomorrow," she left.

As she wended her way through the tables, someone called out her name and she responded, her smile genuine now. She stopped at one table to chat someone up, waved at another person across the café and joked with Katherine Dubowsky, the owner of Coffee's On, while she paid her bill.

Then with a laugh and the tinkle of the door's bell, she was gone.

Rick turned back to his food, feeling curiously deflated, as if the day had lost even more light. He finished his supper quickly, then left for his apartment and his own brand of domestic bliss.

"I don't know if I like the emphasis in this article." Rick pushed the paper across his desk toward Becky and leaned back in his chair, his fingers steepled under his chin. He wore a black cotton shirt today, the sleeves rolled up to his elbows. His usual blue jeans. The subdued morning light highlighted the blond of his hair, shadowed the faint dimple in his cheek. He looked more like the cowboy she had written about in the article, than a publisher of a magazine.

Becky glanced down at the article, wishing for a moment that Rick Ethier weren't so physically appealing. Not because she was attracted to him, mind you, but because the women in the office were starting to annoy her. And it was starting to interfere with her own objectives. She needed people on her side if she was going to maintain a toehold of control over this magazine.

Just this morning she had to listen to Trixie wax eloquent about those eyes, that careless hair. The way he, "well, you know, Becky, kind of strolls. Like he's in charge of his world." Which he was, of course.

Trouble was, it was also her world.

"It's a fairly basic profile. What's the problem?"

Rick rocked a couple of times in his chair, then leaned forward. "Here's the deal. You've got an article about working cowboys who make lousy wages, yet you write it like these guys are the happiest men alive."

"It's what they told me."

"That they were the happiest men alive?"

"That they loved their work. That it wasn't a job as much as a vocation."

Rick acknowledged this with a quick nod. "That may be, but you don't bring up any of the negatives. And don't tell me they didn't talk about any."

"Of course they did. They work long hours. Get hurt a lot. Have to work with rank horses and ornery bosses. As many more of us have to." The words slipped out before she could stop them.

Nice. Nice. Be nice.

"I'm going to take that last comment as a generality." Rick got up from his desk and stood by the window, his hands shoved in the back pockets of his pants. "But none of what you just told me made it into the article."

"That wasn't the point of the article."

Rick turned to her, a dour smile on his face. "And that's my point. You took your own preconceptions to the story and only used facts that worked with what you wanted to show."

Becky didn't have time for this and wondered that he did. She was behind on her own work and phone calls. She knew he was busy consulting with his marketing and focus group on the redesign.

"So what do you want me to do? Rewrite it?" She bit back the anger that was starting up again.

"No. I'd just like to see a bit more balance in what you're doing."

"In keeping with the vision of the magazine," she finished with a light sigh. She wasn't going to concede immediately.

"The vision is more business oriented. As well, I'm

also trying to shape this magazine into a more honest view of life in this part of the country."

"Oh, you made that very clear." Becky stopped. Took a breath. "But business isn't all grimness and focus. There are people who enjoy what they do. I wanted to show that in this article."

"The glass is half-full."

Becky frowned, then caught his inference. "Okay. So I'm an optimist. You say it's half-empty. Neither of us is wrong. It just depends on what you want to focus on." She felt, more than heard, the hardness creeping into her voice and tried to inject a note of humor. "And if you were our art director, you would say we would need a different glass."

Rick frowned. He didn't get it, obviously. "Water management aside, I'd also like to see the article shorter if possible."

"Design will have problems with that."

"We need the space for ads."

"It's a magazine, not a shopping network."

"But ads pay the bills and our salaries."

Becky bit back a comment. In the few days Rick had been here, she realized one thing. Money talked to this man. Loud and clear.

"I'll see what I can do," she said. "Anything else you want to discuss?"

"I'm calling a meeting tomorrow to go over the results of our market survey."

Becky pulled out her Day-Timer and flipped it open to the date. "Sorry. I've got a practice with the children's choir."

"How about after?"

"After, I'm supposed to be meeting with the banner committee to discuss the new designs for the Thanksgiving service in the fall."

Rick drummed his fingers against his thigh. "How about the next night?"

Becky flipped the page and shook her head as she glanced up at Rick.

"Don't tell me," he said, holding his hand up, palm out. "Whatever it is, cancel it. This is important."

Becky stifled a flare of resentment. "So is my meeting."

"Find someone else. This is your job." Rick picked up a folder and flipped it open. "While we're talking about your job, I also want to comment on the lack of letters to the editor."

"People here are generally low-key. If they like something, they don't say anything. If you want a reaction, you have to stir up the nest."

"Not something you're prone to doing." He tilted her a half smile that, in spite of their momentary antagonism, slipped past her defenses and kindled a faint warmth.

"I think I've done a good job."

"But I don't want good," Rick said, holding her gaze. "What I want from you is your best."

Becky frowned, uncomfortable with this new tack. Did he think she was doing a mediocre job? "And that's what you'll get," she said softly. She gathered up her papers and left without another look back, a self-doubt niggling at her confidence.

As she walked down the hall, she reread the article. Had she been overly positive? Had she done a mediocre job?

She thought of the wry grins of the cowboys as they talked about their work. She recognized the griping. Her brothers talked the same way when they had a particularly unpleasant chore. Yet underneath the words, she knew there was a love of a challenge. A pride in their work.

"Hey, Becky, eyes on the road." Cliff caught her by the shoulders and set her aside. He angled his chin toward Rick's office. "Had your bi-hourly meeting with the boss?"

Becky resisted the urge to roll her eyes. Cliff didn't need to see her own frustration. Rick was ruffling all kinds of feathers, but in public she needed to stand behind him. "We had to discuss an article he wants me to look over." Among other things.

Cliff drew her aside and lowered his voice. "Becky, you got to help me. This Rick guy is driving us nuts. He wants us to redo the layout for the next issue. Unless we work 24/7, it's not going to get to the printer on time. Can you make him see sense?"

Becky took a deep breath and drew on the devotions she had read this morning.

"...in humility consider others better than yourselves." She had seldom stumbled over that passage. Until now.

"You know what's at stake here, Cliff. We're in transition." She'd had to face the reality herself. As well, for the sake of unity in the office, she had to at least publicly toe the same line as Rick, though she disagreed with him in private. "It's sort of like sharks. We don't move, we die. And if moving means putting in more hours until we know where this magazine is going, I guess you should return those videos you rented for the weekend." She flashed him a smile, hoping to soften her comment.

Cliff glared at her. Scowled at the door of Rick's office. For a moment Becky thought he was going to charge in and give Rick a blast of his infamous temper.

"It's just for now, Cliff," Becky said, laying her hand on his arm to restrain him. "In a few months it will all settle down."

Cliff's glare shot to her. She smiled back. Held his gaze.

"He wants me to use more stock photos instead of photo shoots for the next issue. How's that supposed to make us stand out from the other magazines?"

Becky gave him a light shake. "It's just for now. Once we get the magazine turning a better profit, you can unleash your creativity once again." She hoped.

Thankfully, his shoulders slumped. He fingered his goatee and Becky knew the moment had passed.

"I'm doing this for you, Becky. Okay? Just so you know."

"Thanks, Cliff."

The door to Rick's office opened and Cliff glanced back over his shoulder at Rick, looking guilty. He flashed Becky a quick grin and ambled back down the hallway.

"Problems?" Rick asked, raising one eyebrow.

"Not anymore." Becky held up the papers. "Got to get back to work here." She scurried down the hallway and ducked into her office. Retreated into her sanctuary to regroup and hoped she didn't have to deal with anyone else's complaints about what was happening at the magazine.

Ever since Rick started, she spent as much of her day calming irate people and putting out fires, trying to be optimistic about what he was doing.

Which she wasn't.

And what kind of reaction were people going to have when Gavin Stoddard started spewing his opinionated coffee-shop talk all over the magazine each month?

Alanna may have been emotional. Gladys may have been anachronistic. But neither generated the kind of mail she was sure Gavin would.

Becky pressed her fingers against her eyelids, pushing back the stress lurching in her midsection. She had head space for only one disaster at a time. And for now, this article took priority.

As she spread the papers in front of her, she felt a twist of frustration. The whole time she was working on the article, she had tried to make sure it was a balanced depiction of what these men did for a living. Yet at the same time she wanted to show their obvious pleasure in their work. Had she been "overly sentimental" again as Rick had once accused her of?

Misgivings slithered through her mind as she read the article through once more. She should listen to the interview tapes again. She had the number of the tape written in her Day-Timer.

Day-Timer. She groaned as she realized where she'd last seen it.

Becky swallowed her pride, got up and walked back to Rick's office. He was on the phone but gestured for her to come in. She pointed to the burgundy folder on the desk and he nodded, not missing a beat in the conversation.

She picked it up and left. But as she closed the door, she caught him looking at her.

And frowning.

Chapter Three

"**H**ow are you enjoying the West?" Colson Ethier's voice sounded overly hearty as if he was trying to inject enthusiasm for his project into his guinea pig.

Rick cradled the phone in the crook of his shoulder as he made some quick notes on one of the papers spread out on the dining room table of his apartment. "The natives are restless and the weather is the pits." Behind him the rain ticked against the glass of the kitchen window, as if testing it. Seeking entry. He had hoped to drive into the mountains this evening and do some photography, but the weather had sent him indoors.

"Have you met Sam and Cora Ellison yet?"

"Grandfather, the extent of my socializing has been to smile at the waitress at Coffee's On." And sitting around an empty apartment on weekends looking over spreadsheets and articles.

"How are you getting along with Becky?"

Rick rapped the table with his pen. "We're not."

A measured beat of silence then, "She's a lovely girl."

She was more than lovely. More than frustrating, too.

"I was hoping you two might get along," Colson continued.

His grandfather sounded pained, and the suspicion that Rick had about Colson's motives was immediately confirmed.

"Editors and publishers aren't supposed to get along." The timer on the microwave went off. "My supper is ready."

"You better go eat then." Colson Ethier paused, cleared his throat as if he wanted to say more. And quickly hung up.

Rick tossed the phone on the couch. "Goodbye to you, too, Grandpa."

Rick couldn't remember his grandfather ever saying goodbye. Since the age of seven, when the death of his mother put him into his grandfather's guardianship, Colson would bring Rick back to the private boys' school he was enrolled in, drop him off and drive away without a backward glance.

The housekeeper told Rick, Colson wasn't comfortable around children, but Rick knew his grandfather was only uncomfortable around him. The evidence of his mother's indiscretion. Consequently Rick and Colson didn't spend a lot of time together, which cut down on the opportunities not to say goodbye.

Once Rick graduated and moved away to college, their farewells were limited to Christmas, Easter and occasionally Thanksgiving. So his grandfather's new interest in Rick's life was too little, too late.

Rick retrieved his dinner from the microwave sat down at the table and set his food in front of him. He paused a moment. Habit, more than anything. Colson

Ethier always prayed before meals and had taught him to do the same. The boarding school he attended tried to instill the same religious beliefs.

After his mother died, Rick didn't trust God much. Living on his own didn't help. When he started traveling and started seeing what the world could be like for people less privileged, cynicism and reality slowly wore away any notions of a loving God in charge of the world.

Rick ate mechanically. The reheated food tasted lousy, but he had eaten so many different kinds of foods in so many different places that he had come to view it simply as fuel. A steady need that had to be responded to at least twice and, if he was lucky, three times a day.

Which reminded him, he had to talk to some of the restaurant owners about participating in a contest he hoped to run in conjunction with the launch of the new magazine. He'd had to scale down his original plan when he sat down with Trixie and the reality of the finances stared him in the face.

He dug through his papers and found his Day-Timer. It felt heavy in his hand and seemed fatter than usual. Frowning, he flipped it open.

The pages were crammed with scribbled notes written in every direction in various shades of ink. Butterfly stickers danced across the page and flowers decorated another. Phone numbers were written sideways.

He flipped back a page, scanning over the dates, trying to make sense of what he read. Was someone at the office playing a practical joke on him?

Then he saw his name, stopped and read, "What am I going to do about Rick?" The question was heavily underlined.

He read the words again, then checked the front of the folder. The initials *R.E.* were imprinted in the soft burgundy leather. He and Becky must have accidentally switched agendas.

Rick glanced over the rest of the pages, looking for other mentions of his name before he realized what he was doing.

Snooping. He closed the book with a guilty flush and set it on the table. He should let Becky know right away he had it. From the look of the jam-packed days, she was going to be lost without it.

"What am I going to do about Rick?"

The words snaked into his mind. Why had she written them?

He went back to the articles Gavin Stoddard had written.

"In order to move into the 'new' market, the Internet market, local business owners will need to rethink their calcified methods of doing business. The name of the game is education, or how to teach an old dog to double-click."

Rick forced himself to concentrate on the rest of the column. But the little leather folder beside him drew his attention like a magnet.

"What am I going to do about Rick?"

What did she think she had to "do"? And what was the problem?

And why did he care?

"...this new way of doing business can be a boon for savvy business owners and a stumbling block to die-hard traditionalists." He continued to scan.

He wasn't a problem that she had to solve, he

thought, throwing down the paper in disgust. He was supposed to be her boss. If there was a problem to be solved, it was his problem with her.

His chair creaked as he pushed himself back from the table, dragging his hands over his face. He had too many things on his mind to be concerned with what his bossy editor thought of him. Tomorrow he was going to be attending a meeting with the chamber of commerce to talk about the magazine and its potential for the town. He had to get a speech ready, a spreadsheet together. He was operating on a shoestring budget and he didn't think he was going to make the ends of the string meet, let alone keep them tied.

He dropped his supper dishes in the dishwasher, tidied the counter then went back into the dining room. As he straightened the papers on the table, he glanced at the burgundy folder again.

And opened it before he could convince himself otherwise.

While his agenda only had a week per page, hers had a page per day and held two months' worth of booklets. Each page was crammed full of notes. She had a busier schedule than the prime minister.

He flipped the pages back to the day they first met, and started reading. "Met Rick Ethier, new boss and old enemy this morning. Too good-looking and I made a fool of myself. Of course I was late for important first meeting."

Rick felt a moment's surprise. He hadn't imagined that brief spark of attraction after all, and the thought kindled a peculiar warmth that was extinguished with the words following. But "old enemy"?

"Got interview with premier." Several exclamation marks followed that one. Obviously excited. "Call secretary and get background information."

"Meeting with Rick. Again." The hard double underline clearly showed her frustration. "Don't like the direction but at least there *is* some. Praying for patience. Constantly."

Prayers again.

He flipped the page over, skimmed over notices to call friends, an appointment with her hairdresser, a meeting that evening at the church, a reminder of another meeting the next night. Wondered who was the Trevor of "Trevor's back," written with a little heart beside it.

"Rick is driving me crazy." No heart beside his name, he thought with a surprising flicker of envy. "He's hired Gavin. Big mistake. Mom and Dad told me I need to pray for him. Said I need to see him as a child of God."

Rick slapped the book shut and pushed himself away from the table. He knew he had made enemies at the magazine. If he'd had a couple of years to make the changes he wouldn't have had to be so aggressive.

He glanced back at the Day-Timer. "I need to see him as a child of God" replayed through his head.

He wasn't a child of God. Wasn't a child of anyone.

He had to return this. Thankfully she'd written two phone numbers inside. No one was at home, so he tried her cell phone.

"Hey there." Becky's voice was almost drowned out by music and voices in the background.

"This is Rick," he said, wondering what place in Okotoks could generate that volume of noise. "I think you've got something of mine."

"Just a sec. Can't hear you." She said something unintelligible. The noise receded and was suddenly shut off. "Sorry about that. Who is this?"

"It's Rick. I think you've got my Day-Timer," he repeated.

"You've accused me of that before, but I'll check." A rustling noise and, "Oh, brother." Deep sigh. "You're right. This isn't good."

She was probably remembering some of the things she had written.

"Where are you now?" he asked. "I could meet you so we can swap." He didn't have time, but a mischievous impulse made him want to see her face when they made the exchange. Impulse and a bit of bruised pride. He didn't usually generate hostility in the women he met.

"I'm at the church, but I can come over."

"No. I'm not doing much. Where's the church?"

She paused and Rick smiled. She was probably squirming in embarrassment. Then she gave him directions which he noted. "See you in a bit," he said with a hearty cheeriness.

A short time later, Rick pulled up to the front of the church, surprised at how large and new it was. Obviously religion went over well in Okotoks. He jogged through the rain, avoiding puddles on the crowded parking lot. The noise he had heard through Becky's cell phone grew as he approached the building.

What was happening on a Friday night at church? The services he occasionally attended with his grandfather were held in a large stately church on Sundays, and as far as Rick knew, not much else happened there.

This place had cars and trucks in the parking lot and

kids running around the outside of the building in spite of the rain that poured down. He opened the large double doors and stepped inside, brushing moisture off his hair and face. A few young kids were hanging around the foyer laughing and roughhousing.

"Thomas, Justin and Kevin. If you're done with youth group, leave. If you're supposed to be practicing, get in there." The woman who spoke was tiny but her authoritative voice even made Rick stop a moment.

"Sorry, Cora," one of the kids said. The teens scampered into the auditorium, letting out another blast of noise as they yanked open the doors.

The woman walked toward him, smiling as she held out her hand. "Naturally I wasn't talking to you. Welcome. I'm Cora Ellison."

Her gray hair was cut bluntly level with her narrow jaw, her hazel eyes laughed up at him. Rick caught glimpses of Becky in the generous mouth and pert nose. He guessed this was Becky's mother. "I'm Rick Ethier," he said, returning her firm handshake.

"Well, now. Finally." Cora took his hand in both of hers, her grin animating her face even more. "I told Becks to invite you over, but she always says you are too busy. And here you are. This is great."

Her exuberant welcome puzzled him. It was as if she knew him, but he doubted her information came from Becky. Not if her Day-Timer were any indication of what she thought of him.

The door beside them opened up and Becky rushed out, her coat flying out behind her, her hands clutching a folder identical to the one in Rick's coat pocket. She saw her mother and veered toward her. "Hey, Mom, I have to step out a moment..." Becky's voice trailed off as her eyes flicked from her mother to Rick. He didn't think he imagined the flush in her cheeks.

"Hello, Becky," he said, tilting a grin her way. "I believe you have something of mine."

Becky looked down at the folder in her hands and her flush deepened. "Yes. Here." She shoved it toward him without making eye contact. Rick slipped it into his pocket.

"You were expecting him, Becky?" Cora Ellison asked.

Becky nodded. "We, uh, accidentally switched Day-Timers." She glanced up at Rick, her expression almost pleading. "Can I have mine back?"

"Oh. Sure." Rick enjoyed seeing Becky a little flustered. It deepened the color of her eyes, gave her an appealing, vulnerable air. But he took pity on her and handed her the leather folder. "Safe and sound." Luckily he wasn't easily embarrassed or he might be flushing, too, knowing he'd read private things.

Becky took it from him and glanced down at it as if to make sure it hadn't been violated. If she only knew.

"Thanks," she said, and was about to turn away when her mother caught her by the arm.

"Becky. Wait a minute. You should have told me Rick was coming." Cora turned to Rick. "Now I can ask you directly. We'd like to have you over for lunch. What about this Sunday? After church?"

Rick stifled a smile at Becky's panicked gaze. He guessed she didn't want him over, which made him want to accept the invitation. "That would be very nice. Thank you."

"I'm looking forward to having you," Cora said, folding her arms over her chest in a self-satisfied gesture. "It will be like the closing of a circle."

Rick frowned at her comment. "What do you mean?"

"Your grandfather lived in Calgary years and years ago. When he was a teenager. Apparently he used to come courting my mother in those days." Cora winked at Rick. "Bet he never told you."

And a few more pieces of the puzzle that was his grandfather fell into place. "No. He never did. Is your mother still alive?"

"More than alive. Right, Becky?" Cora asked, drawing a reluctant Becky into the conversation.

"She's a character, that's for sure," Becky said. She gestured toward the closed doors of the auditorium. "Sorry, but I gotta go," she said vaguely, taking in both her mother and Rick. "Practice."

"I'll see you Sunday," Rick couldn't help but say.

She turned to him, her eyes finally meeting his, her lips drifting up in a crooked smile. "Church starts at ten-thirty. See you then."

He felt a reluctant admiration for how neatly she had cornered him. Church was one of the last places he wanted to be on a Sunday morning, but he couldn't let her get the upper hand. Not after what he'd read. "I'll be here."

She held his gaze, as if challenging him. But when she left, Rick felt a curious reluctance to hang around any longer.

"I should get going, too," he said. "Gotta get ready for tomorrow."

Cora's light touch on his arm surprised him. "I'm looking forward to finding out more about your grandfather. I like a mystery."

"Nothing mysterious about Colson Ethier," Rick said. Except for a twisted desire to send his grandson on a trip down his own particular memory lane. He would be talking to Grandpa Colson as soon as he got a chance. "I'll see you Sunday. Thanks again for the invitation."

Becky tapped her fingers against her chin as she glanced around the foyer of the church once more. Rick better show up soon or she was leaving. When Cora Ellison told her *she* should be the one to make sure he's welcome, Becky only agreed out of a sense of guilt.

She shouldn't have snooped in his Day-Timer. Not that she found anything out. He had a year's worth of dates written in his immaculate handwriting and none were of a personal nature. The only phone numbers were business related. His life looked empty, unappealing and sterile.

"Don't do it, Becks." Leanne, her sister, caught her hand as it edged toward her mouth. "Your nails are just starting to grow back."

"And since when do you care about my nails, Leanne?" Becky said with a quick grin, slipping her sister's arm through hers.

"Since I'm wondering if you're ever going to get a boyfriend again."

"A manicure isn't going to do it and you know it."

"Oh, please, not another 'look not for the beauty nor whiteness of skin' lecture. I get them enough from Mom." Leanne squeezed her sister's arm. "If you spent more time on your hair and makeup, you'd get a guy lickety split."

"That's a little simplistic. Besides, I have lots of guys."

"But they're all just friends," her sister complained.

"I can't believe you don't care about guys. I know Trevor didn't break your heart that much."

"He only dented it a little."

"So why don't you two go out again? I heard he's back."

"Trust me, he'll be gone once the snow flies. I'm not going to date some guy who is just hanging around here, waiting for a chance to leave. This is my home and this is where I want to live."

"If you found the right guy, I'm sure he'd be able to talk you into leaving."

Becky tapped her little sister on the nose. "You see, that's the problem. The right guy for me is one who doesn't want to leave."

Leanne pulled back, frowning. "I think I get it."

"Let me know when you do."

"So how long do we have to wait for this Rick guy?" Leanne said, brushing her long brown hair back from her face. "I promised Donita I'd sit with her."

"Just a few more minutes." Becky glanced at her watch, hoping Rick wouldn't show. Now, or for lunch after church. But what she hoped even more was that he hadn't read her Day-Timer. Like she'd read his.

"Okay, Becks. New guy alert." Leanne tugged on her arm, her eyes riveted to the door. "Shaggy hockey hair. Nice mouth. Gorgeous eyes." Leanne added a dramatic sigh. "He's wearing a suit, but otherwise he's movie-star adorable."

Becky glanced toward the object of her sister's gushing. And straightened as disappointment and a tingle of anticipation flitted through her. Rick's suit gave him an authoritative air at odds with the haircut, or lack of it, that was currently labeled "hockey hair"—long enough to hang out the back of a hockey helmet. "He's also my boss."

Leanne's mouth dropped. "That's Rick Ethier?"

"Let's go say hi and get that part over and done with." Becky snagged her sister's arm, and walked purposefully toward him.

Rick stood in the doorway, looking, she had to concede, a little lost in the wave of people drifting past him.

Someone caught her by the arm, halting her progress. Louise, a woman from one of the committees Becky was involved in. "Becky. Just wanted to know if you've had a chance to go over that banner idea Susan put together."

"Not just yet. I'll check it out this afternoon," Becky said.

"I was thinking we could get your sister to help sew it."

Becky nodded, keeping an eye on Rick.

"Sorry, Louise," Leanne said, rescuing her. "We've got to catch someone before he leaves."

And it looked like he was about to. He had his hand on the door when they caught up to him.

"Good morning, Rick," Becky said, catching his attention. He turned to them and for a moment Becky saw a flicker of an unknown emotion in his blue eyes. Relief? Disappointment?

"Welcome to the service," Becky said with a forced smile. "Mom asked me to make sure you were properly greeted when you came."

Rick smiled back. "Well, tell your mother thanks."

"You can tell her yourself," Leanne said, glancing from Rick to Becky with avid interest. "You're supposed to sit with us."

Becky flashed her sister a warning glance, but Leanne studiously ignored her sister, her entire attention focused on Rick.

"By the way, Rick," Becky said, wishing her sister was more circumspect. "This is my little sister Leanne." Becky put heavy emphasis on "little" hoping she would get the hint.

But Leanne just ignored Becky.

"That's okay. I'm sure I can find a place," Rick said.

"No. Come and sit with us." Leanne touched Rick on the shoulder, winking at Becky. "That way we don't have to find you after church. Makes sense, doesn't it, Becky?"

"Perfect sense," Becky said dryly. "Now we better go."

"Becky is going to be singing in the worship service later on. She's got a great voice," Leanne said as Becky led the way through the crowd.

"I'm looking forward to hearing her," Rick said.

Becky's heart sank at his words. When she had maneuvered him into attending church she had forgotten she would be singing this morning.

And when she saw her family all sitting together, she regretted her impulse even more.

Just about the whole shooting match was watching her as she and Leanne led Rick up the aisle to the empty spot beside her parents. The only ones missing were Colette and her boyfriend, Nick.

"Hey Dad. Mom," Becky said, flashing her brothers and sisters a warning look to dampen their sudden interest in the man behind her. As if that would help. Her family was as curious as magpies and just as nosy. Becky showing up with a man in tow was going to cause a lot of chatter and unwelcome questions.

She dropped onto the pew, and started reading the church bulletin as if trying to show them by her disinterest that he meant nothing.

But Leanne, the little stinker, had positioned Rick so he was sitting right beside Becky.

"Are you going to introduce us?" her father asked, nudging Becky.

Becky looked up at her father with a pleading expression, but his steady gaze reinforced years of ingrained manners. So with a reluctant sigh she turned to Rick, but he was looking away from her.

She touched him lightly on his arm to get his attention. He turned to her then, his eyebrows arched questioningly.

"Rick, I'd like you to meet my father, Sam Ellison. Dad, this is Rick Ethier. And my mother, Cora, you already met."

Cora leaned over and waved, then turned as her attention was drawn by one of the kids behind her. Sam leaned past Becky, shaking Rick's hand. "Pleased to meet you finally. We've heard about you from Becky, of course."

"Really?" Rick's gaze flicked back to Becky, his eyes glinting. "I didn't think she gave me a second thought once she left the office."

Not only second thoughts. Third and fourth ones, as well.

Duty done, Becky returned to her reading. But her entire attention was focused on the man beside her.

Chapter Four

Would he look bored if he crossed his arms?

Rick shifted in his seat, fidgeted, then did it anyway. It had been years since he'd attended church. Not only did he feel out of the rhythm of the church service, he also felt out of place sitting with Becky's obviously close family.

Beside him, Becky leaned forward, her elbows resting on her knees, her chin planted on the palms of her hands, her attention on the preacher. Seeing her head canted to one side and her mouth curved in a half smile, he caught a glimpse of the girl he only saw when she was around other people. She wore a pale blue dress today in some kind of floaty, peasant-looking style. It enhanced the auburn tint of her hair, brought out the peach of her complexion. Pretty in a fun, semiflirty way. Not that she would be flirting with him.

"So I want to encourage all of us to pray for people who hurt us," the minister was saying, and Rick pulled his attention back to the man. "Praying for our enemies frees us from bitterness. From hatred." He paused a moment as if to bring the point home.

"As William Law said, 'There is nothing that makes us love a man so much as prayer for him,'" he continued. "So Christ's command to pray for our enemies is not only for our enemies' good. It is for ours, as well."

Rick looked down at the toes of his shoes as the minister's words pushed him back to his last memory of his mother. She was sitting at a desk in her bedroom, her head bent over a book. When he had asked her what she was doing, she told him she was praying for him.

He looked over at Becky and wondered if she, too, had been praying for him as her parents had suggested. He doubted it.

The congregation got to its feet, breaking off his thoughts.

As the worship group came forward, Becky slipped past him, walked down the aisle and up to the podium. Without any announcement she picked up a cordless microphone, took her position on the stage and cued the group leader with a faint lift of her chin.

The music started quietly, the gentle chords of the piano picking out the melody, the electric organ filling in the spaces.

Becky faced the congregation, waiting as the rest of the musicians joined in. She stood perfectly still, holding the mike with one hand. An overhead light shone brightly on her, singling her out from the rest of the singers. At a pause in the music, she started singing.

Her voice rang clear as the words of an old familiar song poured out of her. "'Our Father, who art in heaven, hallowed be Thy name.'"

Rick recognized the prayer. Had mumbled the words himself as a young boy still trying to please his grandfather.

But he had never heard them sung with such crystal sincerity. He couldn't keep his eyes off Becky as she closed her eyes and her hand lifted up, palm up in a gesture of surrender. She was a woman in communion with her God, her prayer pouring out of her in song, peace suffusing her features.

And as she sang, he heard in the depths of his soul, a still small voice, familiar, yet long suppressed.

The music built as Becky came to the end of the song, her voice growing, filling the building with power and conviction. "'For Thine is the kingdom and the power and the glory...'"

The voice in him grew with the song and for a moment Rick listened. Heard. Then pushed it away.

He and God hadn't spoken in years. What he'd seen in his travels around the world reinforced his opinion that God was disinterested and uninvolved with his creation.

So why am I here? In a place known as God's house?

The last notes of Becky's song died away, and with it, Rick's questions. He was here because he'd been neatly manipulated into coming. No other reason! The minister took the podium again and announced the collection. As the ushers came forward, the tone of the gathering seemed to shift and Rick started to relax.

Ten minutes later, the service was over.

Becky had disappeared from the front of the church, leaving Rick to figure out how to make a graceful exit. But it was not to be.

"Rick, I'd like you to meet the rest of the family," Cora said, catching him by the arm and keeping him anchored to her side. She gestured around the group gathered around her. "The short brunette over there is Treena with her husband, Lyle, and their three children. They live in Okotoks. The long streak of misery beside her is Dennis. One of these days he's going to shave off that shaggy goatee. Beside him is Bert and his girlfriend, Laura. Bert and Dennis work with their father at the orchard. And Leanne you've already met." Cora looked around the cluster of people, her pride evident in her voice and the satisfied smile she bestowed on her brood.

Rick prided himself on his ability to meet people and remember their names, but in the confused conversation that followed Cora's introductions, he lost track of who belonged to who. So he just said a general hello, letting his gaze meet each one of them for a moment.

"Are you still coming for lunch?" Cora asked him as they made their way out of the church building surrounded by chatter and laughter.

"I don't want to intrude," Rick said, feeling he should protest out of politeness, even though a part of him was intrigued by the family's interaction.

"Nonsense." Cora waved off his protestations. "Two people—you'd be intruding. With ten, you're hardly a blip on the radar. Now, where did that Becky go?" Cora looked around, frowning. "Leanne, do you mind riding with Rick to show him the way to our place?"

Cora patted Rick on the arm in a maternal gesture that made him smile, threw out a flurry of instructions to the rest of the family and headed off, leaving a slightly breathless Rick in her wake.

Leanne followed him outside to his Jeep, frowning as he unlocked it. "From the way Becky talked about you, I figured you'd be driving some kind of fancy convertible."

"And how did she talk about me?" Even as he spoke,

he was sorry he asked. What Becky said about him out of the office wasn't any of his business. Bad enough that he had read her private thoughts about him already.

Leanne shrugged, flipping down the visor on the passenger side. "I dunno," she said, running the tip of her finger over her eyelid. "She just made you sound, you know, like some kind of rich, spoiled guy who traveled a lot."

"She got the traveling part right," Rick said dryly as he maneuvered his way out of the parking lot.

"You mean you're not rich?" Leanne asked, finger-combing her hair away from her face. "I thought your grandfather had tons of money."

"Grandfather isn't short of cash. But the only way I can get any of it, if I were to want any of it, is to join the Ethier empire. And I'm not about to put my head in that noose." He stopped and turned to Leanne. "Where am I supposed to be going, Navigator?"

"Head out of town on the main drag, then hang a left at the red horse barn." Leanne dug through her purse and pulled out a package. "Some gum?"

He turned and started driving. "How far is this red horse barn?"

"Not far." Leanne frowned as she popped the gum into her mouth. "Hey, slow up," she said, pointing out a girl walking down the sidewalk of the road they were driving down. "There's Sharelle. Can we pick her up? She hasn't been to my place in, like, forever."

"Your mom won't mind having unexpected company?" Rick asked as he pulled over on the road, pulling up beside a petite girl with short black hair and coffee-colored skin.

Leanne threw him a puzzled look. "Sharelle's my friend."

He presumed that put her in a category other than "company."

Leanne rolled down the window and stuck her head out.

"Hey, Sharelle," Leanne called, waving to her friend. "Coming over?"

"Who you with?" Sharelle asked, walking up to Leanne's window. She bent over, glancing in at Rick. "Hey there," she said, flashing him a grin.

"This is Rick. He works with Becky. He came to church with us this morning. Get in."

"I'll have to call my mom when we get to your place. I don't have my cell with me," Sharelle said, climbing into the back seat, looking around the back of the Jeep. "Nice wheels."

Leanne turned to Rick. "Do you have a cell phone she can use?"

Rick handed it to her. "No problem."

"Good thing we weren't riding with Becky," Leanne said, her tone clearly indicating that this was not a compliment. "She hardly ever packs her cell with her. Can't figure that. If I had a cell phone, I'd have it with me all the time."

"Yah, and you'd be talking on it all the time, wouldn't you?" Sharelle's voice rose at the end of each of her sentences, as if in question while she punched in her parents' number.

Leanne shifted sideways, looking back at her friend. "Did you talk to her about helping with the youth retreat?"

Sharelle flipped her hand toward Leanne. "Said she had some important interview that day? With the premier?"

Rick's heart kicked up a notch in a mixture of pleasure and anger. Becky hadn't told him that she'd final-
ized a date for the interview. If Sharelle hadn't casually
dropped that little tidbit in conversation he wondered if
Becky would have even bothered to let him know.

"When is your retreat?" he asked, trying to keep his
tone casual.

"Long weekend in September?" Sharelle smiled at
him, then started talking to her mother on the phone.

Rick hoped she was telling and not asking as he made
a mental note of the date. He wasn't going to say anything right away to Becky. Better that he bide his time
and see what she did with the information.

"You have to turn up ahead," Leanne said, pointing
to a large red building close to the road. "Go to the end
of the road and you'll go straight into Mom and Dad's
driveway. We're probably first so if you don't want to
get, like totally sandwiched between cars, you might
want to park by the barns."

Rick took Leanne's advice and parked a ways away
from the house in the lee of a large brown building. He
followed Leanne and Sharelle up the driveway and
through an ivy-covered archway granting them entrance
to a spacious yard sheltered by trees. His step slowed
on the brick walk as his gaze was caught by the vibrant
flowers cascading out of pots hanging from the eaves
of the porch, spilling out of endless flower beds border-
ing an emerald-green lawn and tucked up against the
house. Flagstone walkways branched off the main one
meandering past a plant-filled pond with a fountain only
to disappear around the front of the house. Closer to the
house two wooden slatted benches flanked by huge

flowerpots extended an unspoken invitation to sit and enjoy the symphony of color and light that filled the yard surrounding the large two-story farmhouse.

"Your mother must love gardening," Rick said, stopping to look around.

"This is Dad's thing," Leanne said, glancing back over her shoulder at Rick. "He spends almost as much time here as he does in the orchard."

Rick had seen a lot of professionally landscaped yards of friends of his grandfather but none created this welcoming atmosphere.

The door opened and Sam Ellison stepped out onto the deck. "Hey, Sharelle," he said with a booming voice, giving the girl a one-armed hug. "Good to see you. You and Leanne can help Mother with lunch."

Sam beckoned Rick with his large hand. "Come in. Cora has coffee on."

"I was just admiring your yard. It's amazing." Rick took another look around the yard. "Did you do all this yourself?"

"I built on what Cora's parents started. They planted the trees and I added the rest. Do you want a tour?"

"You'll never get coffee," Leanne warned. "Maybe not even lunch."

"Don't you and Sharelle have work to do?" Sam said, giving them a gentle push toward the door.

Leanne gave Rick a quick smile, whispered something to Sharelle. They disappeared into the house.

Sam rolled his eyes as the door slapped shut behind them. "Teenage girls," he said in a tone that summed up all the confusion and exuberance of that age and sex.

The crunch of tires on the gravel made Rick glance

behind him. Three cars pulled up, stopped and people spilled out of them all, laughing and noisy. One of them was Becky.

He wasn't sure he was ready to face the Ellison family en masse, nor to see Becky in a more casual setting. He kept remembering her solo at church. And her sincerity. "I'd love to look around some more," Rick said.

"Would give the noise level a chance to settle down," Sam said, following Rick's gaze. "I'll show you the lilies first. They're around front."

As Sam led the way, Rick chanced one more quick glance back over his shoulder. Becky was watching him, her forehead seamed in a frown.

"Did you check the messages, Becky?" Cora asked, giving the pot of soup on the stove another stir. "Trevor called. Said he was back in the country."

"I saw." Becky started slicing open the homemade buns her mother had laid out on the counter.

"You going to call him back?"

Becky shook her head. "I'll connect some other time."

Cora tasted her soup and grinned at her daughter. "He sounded lonely. I always liked Trevor."

"He's a nice guy. Just got itchy feet is all."

"Not all men are like your father and brother-in-law—more than willing to stay in one place all their lives. You might have to rearrange your standards."

"I like Okotoks. And I like living in a small town where I know everyone. Where I can be involved."

"A bit too involved," Cora muttered.

Becky chose to ignore that comment. "Where's the butter?"

Cora handed Becky the foil-wrapped block. "Did you hear that Yvonne and Randy are engaged?"

"Yes. Her mother told me at the library board meeting a few weeks ago." Becky peeled the foil back and started spreading.

"And I saw Deb and Gordon in church together."

"They've been dating for a while now. Deb said they were going to move to Calgary as soon as she's done school." Becky wished her mother would stop this litany of the dating game. It only underscored her own single state and made her feel like a loser. Which she knew she wasn't. She had made her own choices. That most of the eligible young men from Okotoks chose to move away was their problem, not hers.

"Deb said she had a cousin who was coming up to stay for a bit. He's single."

"And you're being very obvious, Mother." Becky didn't even look up from her work. "You know I've got other things on my mind."

"Like your writing? You haven't spent that much time on it lately."

"Been busy."

"Like I said."

"I can't just turn the creativity on and off, Mom. And lately it feels like it's been off."

"Why lately?"

Becky dug into the butter, scooping way too much. "Lately," she thought, because Rick Ethier suddenly showed up in my life. The man who hated my book and let everyone who subscribes to his grandfather's magazine know why. That's why "lately."

"Just not inspired."

Cora folded her elbows on the counter and leaned close to her daughter. "You should ask Rick to help you with it. He's a good writer."

Right.

"Rick is busy turning the magazine around. I doubt he has time for much else." Or interest. Becky dropped another buttered bun into the large metal bowl beside her.

"He seems like a nice man."

"Code for 'Why aren't you interested?'"

"That's not what I meant." Her mother faked an innocent smile and Becky decided to humor her.

"News flash, Mother. He's only here until he can get the magazine going in a direction that will make enough money so that he can get out of town as fast as his Jeep's wheels will turn. He's temporary. So he's not my type and I'm not his."

"Well, for now you can go rescue your boss from your father. Tell them lunch is ready," Cora said.

Becky glanced out the large picture window beside her at the two men wandering across the yard. Sam was tall but Rick's blond head topped him by an inch. Now and again Rick would nod and laugh, his smile flashing like a beacon. "I'm busy," Becky said.

"I can do it," Leanne said, popping her head into the kitchen.

"Go for it, Leanne," Becky said. She was only too glad to relinquish the job to her sister. Leanne was obviously far more interested in Rick than she was.

"Becky will go," Cora said, giving Becky her "don't argue with me look" honed and perfected over years of raising six children. Becky knew better than to challenge it.

Rick and Sam were crouched down by a young maple tree. The low murmur of her father's voice was steady, and Becky could hear Sam eagerly inducting Rick into the intricacies of the flora on the yard.

"It's like a highway," Sam was saying, his hand waving up and down along the trunk of the tree. "The ants go up the tree to the new growth here." He pushed himself to his feet and pulled down a branch. "This is where the aphids are. They milk the aphids and then go scurrying down the trunk to the ant colony with the milk past the others that are going up. An amazing small part of how God works everything together. Fascinating, really."

Becky had always thought so and used to spend hours as a child patiently watching the ants' progress on other maple trees. She couldn't imagine that Rick was even remotely interested.

But he was politely looking closer at the branch, angling his head to the side as if to see better, his hair falling aslant. He looked relaxed and was smiling. And for a split second she felt a tug of attraction. Then he looked up at her and the smile disappeared.

And that bothered her more than she liked to admit.

Sam caught the direction of Rick's gaze. "Come to fetch us, Becks?"

"Orders from the high command. 'Go ye therefore into the yard and rescue Rick,' or something like that." Becky curled her arm through her father's.

Sam shrugged, his smile taking in Rick and Becky. "Cora is deathly afraid that someday I'm going to bore some very polite visitor to death and then we'd have some explaining to do when the coroner shows up."

"I could think of worse places to breathe my last,"

Rick said easily. "You've created a small paradise here." He looked relaxed with his tie hanging out of the pocket of his suit coat. The top button of his shirt was unbuttoned and he looked more at ease than he had this morning in church.

"I was taught that God reveals himself to us through the Bible and creation," Sam continued as they started toward the house. "I like to think of my gardening and orchard work as part of my worship to him."

Rick's face tightened and for a moment Becky thought he was going to argue with her father. He caught Becky's gaze, then looked away. She wondered what he was going to say and almost wished he had voiced his opinion. She knew so little about him.

And had found out even less, snooping through his stark, empty Day-Timer.

The blush that warmed her neck had nothing to do with the warmth of the sun and everything to do with her guilt at the thought of looking through his private papers. Thankfully she had discovered nothing personal or she would have felt even more self-conscious.

"You're mighty quiet, Becky," Sam said. "That's not like my girl at all."

Becky wrinkled her nose at him. "Maybe I'm trying to give my new boss a good impression, Dad."

"Too late for that. Isn't it, Rick?" Sam said, pulling Becky close to his side as the walked up the wooden steps. "My Becky is so transparent, I'm sure you know everything about her already."

"I hope not," Rick said, holding open the screen door of the house.

Becky caught his eyes as she walked past him and

wondered what he meant by his comment. Then decided she didn't want to know.

"Okay, everyone, Dad is here. Let's start," Cora announced, clapping her hands to get her family's attention.

Everyone gathered in the kitchen, forming a loose circle. Becky bit back a smile at Leanne's obvious maneuvering to get beside Rick.

"Let's pray," Sam said, glancing around the circle. This was the signal for everyone to take the hand of the person beside them. Rick looked a little baffled.

"We usually hold hands while we pray," Becky said. "But if you're uncomfortable with that, we can forget it."

"No. That's fine. Don't change anything on my account." Rick took Leanne's hand, flashed her his most charming smile and lowered his head.

The brief spurt of jealousy Becky felt was as sudden as it was surprising.

Her father started praying, his deep voice thanking God for the day. For the church service. For the food they were about to eat. He prayed for each family member, for the community and for the government of the country.

"And as we come to you, Lord, we want to especially pray for those who have hurt us. Those whom we see as our enemies. Help us, Lord, to see them as You see them. To love as You love. In Your name, amen."

Becky kept her head lowered a moment, trying to take her father's words into her heart. Rick wasn't her enemy per se. Her opponent maybe. Someone she'd had a hard time thinking charitably about even before he was her boss.

Please, Lord, help me to care about him as a person.

Help me to want only good for him and to forgive him, she added silently.

She raised her head, catching Rick's eyes on hers. As she gave him a tentative smile, she was surprised to see one in return. It was a start.

Of what, she didn't know.

Chapter Five

"So my challenge to businessmen in Okotoks clinging tenaciously to archaic ways of doing business is find a way to tap into a broader market...."

Becky dropped the page and her elbows onto her desk and clutched her hair, pulling it loose from her ponytail.

Tenacious. Archaic. Could Gavin Stoddard have found more inflammatory language to convey his point? The magazine was going to be flooded with angry letters all addressed to "The Editor." Editor being Becky Ellison, innocent bystander.

She carefully shuffled the papers in order to tamp down her own emotions.

Her anger surfaced so quickly these days, the result of working too many long hours switching the magazine's focus midstream. When she had agreed to help with the youth program, she hadn't counted on her well-ordered work life getting swirled and rearranged by Rick's whirlwind plans.

Work was taking up more and more of her time as she ran interference for an owner bound and determined to turn this magazine around on a dime, disgruntled staff notwithstanding.

Cliff was complaining about budget restraints. Trixie about the diminishing bank balance. Becky would have loved to complain to someone, but her only recourse was Rick.

The reason for the general air of discontent around the office.

Becky flipped Gavin's first column back and carefully read over the second one, just to reassure herself that she wasn't overreacting.

"...we need to get with the program. Stop thinking that if we are here, people will come..."

Nope. Just as bad.

She walked down the hallway to Rick's office, took a deep breath and knocked lightly. Without waiting for an answer she slipped inside.

Rick was on the phone, pacing back and forth, talking quietly. But Becky heard the now-familiar edge on his voice. The way he was tugging on the hair at the back of his neck wasn't a good sign, either.

Looked like she was facing an uphill battle even before she started.

Rick nodded curtly. "I'll keep it in mind, Grandfather." He stood in front of the window, one hand on his hip, his knuckles white on the handset.

"No. I'll stick this through to the end on my own. I don't want any money coming in that the magazine hasn't earned."

Speak for yourself, Becky thought, remembering Cliff and Trixie. The magazine needed a serious injection of cash.

"You don't need to come down and check on me. I'll do this on my own, okay?" Rick sighed and lowered the phone. Becky heard the light beep as he disconnected without saying goodbye.

He stared at the handset for a moment, his eyes narrowed, then, with deliberate motions, he hung it up in the cradle. When he looked up at Becky, she almost recoiled at the banked anger in his eyes.

"What can I do for you?"

Becky's heart did a slow flop, then began racing.

"I thought you heard my knock...." She gestured futilely back at the door. "I'm sorry I interrupted.... I'm too used to coming and going like when Nelson..." She bit her lip on her next words.

"I'm not Nelson, am I?"

"No you're not, and I'm sorry." She gave him a tentative smile that bordered on insincere. But she hoped that the outward action would bear inward fruit and soften her heart toward him.

Her mind flicked back to Sunday as she noted his hostile body language. For a few hours at her parents' place she had seen him relaxed and, she thought, enjoying himself with her family. She'd even heard him laugh out loud when Dennis told his infamous Jean Chrétien joke. He'd teased Leanne, putting her completely under his spell. Her father also thought he was very charming and when Rick left, Sam had asked Becky why she had such a hard time with him.

They would know if they saw him now. Today he looked like the other Rick's evil twin.

She picked the papers up off the desk. "I'll come another time. When you're ready to talk instead of interrogate."

Rick's eyebrows snapped together. "What do you mean?"

"I'd like to discuss something with you. Not fight it out. It can wait." It couldn't, really. Gavin's column was set to run in the following issue. But she wasn't going to antagonize Rick when he was already so obviously upset.

"No. Sit down. If you've got a problem, I want to deal with it right away."

Becky bit her lip as she laid Gavin's column down again. She didn't sit, preferring to face Rick on her feet. Not that it gave her much of a tactical advantage. He topped her by at least five inches.

"I'm concerned with the language Gavin uses in this column."

Rick tunneled his hands through his hair, clutching the back of his neck as his eyes bored into hers. "I thought you would be."

"And that didn't count?"

"Becky, this guy knows his stuff. He's laying out a challenge to the local businesses. We need to give them tangible information they can use."

"But not this man and not this way." Becky spun the paper around and started reading randomly. "'...burying your head in the sand...outmoded or nonexistent business plans...'" She looked up at Rick. "This is not the language of community. It doesn't build up, it breaks down."

Rick dropped his hip on the edge of the desk, crossing his arms. "Let me guess. You've been reading books on building self-esteem."

"What I've been doing is living in a community that

deserves to be treated with respect. And this—" she poked her finger at the article "—doesn't do that."

"In order for this magazine to succeed we need to look beyond this community. To other towns that are on the edge of Calgary who are struggling with the same issues. Maybe they do need to take a hard look at themselves." Rick swung his leg, his movements punctuating his comments.

Becky felt her hold on the discussion slowly slipping as she recognized the reality of what Rick was saying. Yet, she knew that she was also right.

"So telling local shop owners and businesses that they are dumb and 'archaic' is going to get them to listen to Gavin's brave new vision for Okotoks and other smaller towns?" Becky walked past Rick to the window overlooking the street, as if drawing strength from the community laid out below her. "These people down there know more than anyone else what they are facing. Rubbing their noses in it isn't going to sell this magazine."

Rick pushed himself off his desk, and as he came to stand behind Becky she caught a vague hint of his aftershave and soap, felt the warmth of his chest close to her back. He was too close but she suppressed the urge to move away. To do so would be to admit his dominance over her.

"But giving them practical advice will help sell the magazine," he said, his voice quieter now. "People will respond to that."

Becky turned to face him. Mistake. She had to look up to catch his eyes. And as she did, she noticed the change. In spite of the fact that she was arguing with him, his anger had dissipated and in their blue depths she caught a glint of humor.

He's enjoying this, she thought with a start. I'm trying to defend a sensible and practical position and he's laughing at me.

She crossed her arms tightly over her chest as if holding back her rising frustration. "What people will respond to is the underlying tone of Gavin's article. Superiority."

"I think you're being overly sensitive."

Rick's words were waved in front of her like a gentle taunt. She swallowed back her response. And tried smiling again.

"I take it you're going to run Gavin's article no matter what I say."

Rick nodded. Decisively.

"Then I have nothing more to say," she said, slipping past him. She gathered up the papers and tapped them into a neat pile, buying herself some time. Surprisingly she felt reluctant to leave. She had foolishly hoped her opinion would have counted for something but she couldn't throw out the words that would make him understand.

She glanced one more time back up at him and as their eyes met, she felt it again. That peculiar feeling of connection.

The ring of the phone broke the moment and Becky turned to leave.

"Well, hello, Mrs. Ellison."

In spite of herself Becky spun back.

Rick held her gaze while he listened, a smile teasing one corner of his mouth. "Sure. I'd love to come for dinner. Next week Saturday should be fine."

Becky's heart did a slow flip. Since Rick had started working, her home had become a refuge for her. A place she could simply be herself without having to force her smiles.

Now it seemed her mother was determined to practice the Christian hospitality that Becky was reluctant to extend to her boss.

"Thanks for the invite. I'll see you next week." Rick put the phone back in the cradle and grinned toward Becky. "You look a little disgruntled," he said.

"Just plain gruntled," she returned with calculated crispness. "I was hoping you would reconsider the Gavin articles." Which wasn't the full reason for her momentary funk. She was gone this weekend with her children's choir and was hoping for some time with just her family next weekend.

"I'm going to run the articles," Rick said, his tone taking on the edge that Becky recognized all too well. "Just make sure you don't edit the life out of 'em."

"And you make sure you're on hand with the shields when the rotten tomatoes come sailing in."

"When life throws you tomatoes, make salsa," he quipped with a crooked grin.

Becky resisted the urge to roll her eyes. At least he was in a better mood than when she came in. Thank goodness for that.

"Before you go, I want you to empty a couple of days in your busy schedule next month." Rick rifled through one pile of papers on his tidy desk and pulled one out. "The owners of the Triple Bar J are putting on a fund-raising ride and were hoping we could do a feature article on it."

"When?"

"The third week of the month."

Becky's mind scrambled through her schedule. "I can't tell you until..."

"You check out your schedule. The ride is a whole week, but I told them we could go in with them one day and out the next. So it would be two days."

"I'll let you know."

"Soon. I don't want to miss this chance."

"I thought we were getting away from cows and farmers." The words slipped past her lips before she even realized she had spoken.

Rick shot her a penetrating look. "Triple Bar J is part of the holdings of a much larger entity. Get them and we've got a good 'in' on a corporate market." He waved the paper slowly, as if thinking, his eyes holding hers. "They've already expressed a great deal of interest in the article we're going to be doing on the premier. Said they want to be a part of that issue. You have that under control, don't you?"

Becky squirmed a little. She'd had a firm commitment from the premier's office for a while now. She knew she should have told Rick but was hoping she could hold off long enough so he would end up getting too busy to help her with it. "Yes, I do."

"And it's an exclusive?"

"Of course." She stifled her immediate resentment. "Otherwise what would be the point? Any one of the dailies would scoop us."

"Good. Then all we have to do is get this account with Triple Bar J and this magazine will be on the upward swing." He slapped his hand against the paper in triumph and flashed her a wide smile. "And the sooner that happens, the sooner I'm out of here."

"That's not going to happen in one issue," Becky retorted. "Or two or three. Our cost overrun is getting a little scary, what with the market survey and all the extra promotion we're doing."

"It will pay back."

Becky wasn't so sure. And he didn't want to take any money from Grandfather Colson. Of course, what did it matter to Rick whether the magazine made money or not? One way or the other he had a ticket out of here.

Back in her office she flipped open her agenda to see if she could squeeze two days out of the week Rick wanted her on the trail ride.

Notes and scribbles filled all available space before and after.

A thread of panic spiraled up within her as she looked at her full days and evenings. She had promised her editor that she would have a proposal in his hands in a couple of months. All she had so far was a rough idea and a lot of scratched-out writing. She thought she had given herself lots of time. But as she flipped through the weeks ahead she could see chunks of time gobbled up by work and other activities, some doubling up.

You don't find time... You make time. She remembered Rick's words.

That was all well and good, but how? She needed this job and she had other responsibilities in the church that she couldn't shirk. God had given her many gifts and she didn't feel right if she didn't use them.

She had already cancelled a meeting for tomorrow

night because Rick wanted to discuss the new layout of the magazine with Design. That was a guaranteed three-aspirin meeting. Cliff had been haranguing her for the past week about taking care of him. And Rick was going to talk about using stock photos for the next few issues.

Blessed are the peacemakers, Becky thought, pushing her Day-Timer aside.

She started in on Gavin's article. It grated even harder on closer reading. Easy for Rick to approve this veiled rant at the businesses of Okotoks. He was going to be out of here as soon as possible. She deleted a few of the more offensive adjectives. Hardly editing the life out of them, as Rick had warned her, but hardly the damage control she had hoped to inflict.

She wound a bit of hair round her finger as she mentally ticked off her options. Edit it to her standards and run the risk of getting Rick riled up?

Run it with a disclaimer so she could at least look her fellow community members in the eye?

Or offer an alternative.

As the last thought slipped lightly into her mind, Becky caught it. Another column. Something positive. Upbeat and uplifting. And done free of charge.

She knew exactly who could do it.

Rick flipped through the binder holding the final proof of the magazine. From here, the first new and improved *Going West* would head to the printer. "Looks good, Cliff. I like the new font and the spacing is very pleasing. What do you think, Becky?"

Becky tapped her pencil against her lip as she studied the mock-up in front of her. This new issue of *Going*

West had a sharper edge. The headlines were punchier, the pictures bolder.

It was still a shock to see huge blocks of ads cutting into the articles and marching down the sides of pages. Rick and his sales staff had been busy little beavers to garner this much extra advertising in such a short while.

"It's definitely moving in the direction you're headed," she said, hoping her words sounded more encouraging than she felt.

"When will we be moving away from the stock photos?" Cliff asked, his chair creaking out his annoyance.

"When we start to pull out of our overdraft."

"Which will happen when?"

Thankfully Rick ignored Cliff's belligerence. "It will take a few issues. I'm pinning a lot on our October issue." Rick threw Becky a sidelong glance. "Becky and I are going to be covering the Triple Bar J Western Ride and we'll get you some photos you can work with."

"But those photos won't work for fall."

"We're not going to be as seasonal as we would like, but it's an interesting topic and I'm hoping we'll get some great pictures," Becky said, frowning a warning at Cliff. Looked like she was going to have another hand-holding session with him after this meeting.

"Who's going to be taking those?" Cliff asked, his voice a study in peevishness.

"I will," Rick said. "And the article is as much about the ride as an advertorial for the Triple Bar J," Rick continued.

The heavy silence that followed his comment said more than any complaint or protest could have.

Becky flipped to another page in the binder, past Gavin's article, the sound swishing through the quiet. "You've done a good job with the layout," Becky said to Cliff, her small peace offering. "It has an energy the other issues didn't."

"Thanks, Becks." Cliff accepted her praise with a crooked grin. "I put this new column you gave me opposite Gavin's, like you suggested."

"What column?" Rick flipped the page, as well, frowning.

Becky rocked lightly in her chair to cover her sudden flip of nerves. "We had to hold back the article slated for that page. It didn't fit in size and content. I had to make a last-minute decision on this column. Might turn it into a regular."

"'Runaround Sue'?" Rick's tone didn't bode well. "Who is she and why isn't there a picture with the byline?"

"Sue prefers to remain anonymous for now. And I respect that."

Rick glanced down at the article and heaved a sigh as he started reading aloud. "'He's a man with a mission,'" Rick read. "'With single-minded attention he tears down the road, accelerator pushed to the limit, unafraid of what the journey might bring him. He dares all challenges and laughs at danger. He has youth. He has energy.'" Rick paused at the paragraph break. "'He has his father's truck.'" Rick looked up from the binder, shaking his head. "What is this about and why wasn't I consulted?"

Because you'd probably have vetoed it.

"When Cliff showed me the mock-ups I realized we would either have to split the original article twice or come up with something shorter. I figured this would work better. It's light and balances Gavin's column." Becky paused and delivered her strongest shot. "And Sue is doing this gratis for now." Which was a small point given the declining financial situation.

Rick jerked his chin toward her. "I don't know if I like the direction. Family humor?"

"Light humor," Becky corrected. "A kind of positive note to lighten things up a bit. Everyone likes to smile. Chuckle a little."

Rick blew out a sigh and caught his lower lip between his teeth. He wasn't pleased, but Becky knew that any change at this stage would cause expensive delays.

"We'll run it for now," he conceded, slapping the binder shut. "The rest looks great, everyone. Good job. Let's get this to the printer."

In the shuffle to leave, Becky winked at Cliff, thankful for Rick's sudden affirmation.

"Becky, I need to talk to you before you leave," Rick said as Becky got up.

She sank back into her chair, stifling a groan. While she waited for Cliff to leave, she managed not to tap her fingers on the arm of the chair or swing her foot in impatience. She had a meeting at the church in fifteen minutes.

Rick waited by his desk until the door closed behind the last person. Once again he perched on the edge of his desk. Once again he crossed his arms over his chest.

"A quick note to let me know what you were doing with this 'Runaround Sue' would have been in order here."

She knew he was right, but she also knew it would have been an uphill battle to convince him to run it. Apologizing took less time than asking permission.

"I'm sorry," she said, holding his steady gaze. "You're right."

Rick's eyes took on an inward look. "Why won't you tell me who Sue is?"

Becky released the tension in her shoulders with a slow "what can I do?" shrug. "She prefers to remain anonymous."

"As well, I gave you Gavin's next four columns. I think you could afford me the same courtesy."

"I'll get them to you as soon as she gets them to me." She pulled the binder close and scooted to the edge of her chair. "Is that all?"

Rick stroked his chin with his thumb, his lips flirting with a smile. "Why do I get the feeling that you're hiding something?"

"Because you don't trust people."

Becky slapped her fingers to her mouth as if to stop them, but it was too late. The words were out, hanging between them like a taunt.

"Maybe I've had reason not to," he said before she had a chance to apologize.

His abrupt turn away from her was a classic signal for her to leave and time was ticking. But in his words Becky caught the vaguest hint of sorrow.

"Why not?" She asked the question quietly, hoping to offset the callousness of her previous comment.

Rick glanced back over his shoulder, as if surprised she was still there. He held her curious gaze a moment. "Trust is a relationship," he said finally.

"I'm sure moving around all the time doesn't help you build relationships."

"It suits me."

"And what if you meet someone special? Don't you think you'll want to settle down then?"

Rick shrugged, his charming smile back in place. "Hasn't happened yet, so I don't need to make that kind of decision, do I?"

"But you might."

"I doubt it. Most women like their men to put down roots. I can't think of any reason I'd want to do that."

Becky thought of his empty Day-Timer and his lack of connections. A quick glance around his office reinforced that. Nelson had had pictures of his family and holidays decorating most of the walls and jostling for space on his desk. Her own office held pictures of nieces, nephews, brothers, sisters, parents, friends. She was running out of room on the bulletin board for more photos.

Rick's desk held only papers and the walls were still bare. Not a photograph or snapshot in sight.

She felt a flash of pity and sorrow.

"I hope you change your mind someday," she said as she got up. "I believe we all need a place to call home."

Rick held her gaze a moment, his blue eyes delving deep into hers as if searching out her secrets. "And why do you care, Rebecca Ellison?"

She couldn't look away, and as the moment lengthened, an indistinct emotion shifted deep within Becky and she felt herself softening toward him. "Because I believe you are also a child of God."

Rick laughed, cynicism edging the sound. "I'm nobody's child, Becky. Least of all God's."

And of all the things he said, that was the saddest of all.

Chapter Six

"Before I leave, I thought I'd get you the rest of the mail," Trixie said, dropping a bundle of opened letters onto Becky's desk. Becky flipped through them with one hand while she ate her sandwich with the other. She had spent the entire day running around and had just come into the office to answer a few phone messages and chase down a couple of articles for the next issue. Somewhere in all of the mess that was turning out to be her evening, she had to find a chance to work on another "Runaround Sue" column and get to a meeting with the youth pastor.

"The magazine has only been out a week. We've never gotten this kind of response before," Becky mumbled, wiping the crumbs with the cuff of her shirt.

"Most of them are from businesses. Most of them look handwritten." Trixie pursed her lips. "I sorted them into positive and negative but overall, I'd say not good."

Becky skimmed the first one, mentally separating herself from the anger spilling out on the pages. Countless times her father had told her not to take the letters personally. She tried, but she had a long ways to go before harsh words didn't give her a clench in the pit of her stomach and a desire to go running to the writer to apologize for anything that might have caused offense.

"Has Rick seen these?"

"He's at a Rotary Club meeting. Didn't think he'd be back at the office tonight."

"I guess I'll wade through these then, once I'm done working on this profile." She was also going to have to phone the church and tell the youth pastor she wouldn't be making the meeting tonight. Which also meant she wouldn't have time to work on her book proposal. She pushed down a beat of resentment. Work was taking up too much time. And most of the work was thanks to Rick. "Thanks, Trixie. I'll see you tomorrow."

"You sure you don't want any help?"

Becky shook her head and finished her sandwich in one bite. "There's not really a lot you can do, but thanks."

"See you tomorrow then." Trixie left, and the silence that followed her was a blessing.

Hours later Becky pushed herself away from her desk and stretched her arms above her head with a yawn. The pieces were edited and she had chosen some of the more articulate letters for print in the magazine. That most of them were negative was not her problem.

"Runaround Sue" had proven surprisingly easy to write. Now, at nine o'clock at night, her day was officially over.

She switched off her computer and reveled in the quiet. During the day, the office was a hive of voices and telephones and keyboards clacking. The silence that enveloped her was a relief. A chance to let her busy mind slow down and empty out.

Tomorrow would bring another set of last-minute disasters and changes and juggling finances, but for now her day was over.

She glanced out the window of her office at the setting sun and stifled a moment of frustration. During the short days of winter she looked forward to the longer daylight hours of summer. But now that they'd come, she spent most of them inside. She'd had also only a few hours last week to work on her latest book but all she had to show for it was two more pages of drivel. She was never going to get it done if Rick kept piling on the work.

Yawning, she snagged her sweater off the back of her chair and threaded her arms through the sleeves. She had dressed up today—her favorite pink shirt and denim skirt—for one of her meetings. She had also vaguely hoped that Rick could see that she didn't always wear jeans and T-shirts. But he had been gone all day.

The click of the back door opening was like a shot scattering panic through her body.

Footsteps down the hallway, easy, measured, sent her heart thumping against her ribs. Who was here this time of the night? What did they want?

"Is that you, Becky?"

Relief made Becky sag against her chair.

"Yes, it is, Rick. Come on in."

The door opened and Rick stood framed by the doorway, his eyes flicking over her office, as if making sure. "I thought you had a meeting tonight?"

"I skipped it to work on this. What are you doing out?"

"My Jeep broke down a few blocks from here." Rick stepped into her office, pulled his tie off and tucked it into his pocket. He ran his hands through his neatly combed hair and completed his transformation from stiff businessman to Rick. "My cell phone died so I thought I'd call from the office."

"There's no garage open this time of night. But I could give you a ride home if you want."

Rick shrugged. "No need to go out of your way."

"I truly don't mind." She flashed him a faint smile, then got up from behind the desk.

"There's no rush. You can finish up."

Becky glanced back at the papers on her desk, feeling a flicker of shock. Her "Runaround Sue" column lay on top of the pile. "I'm pretty much done here," she said, shuffling the papers to hide the evidence. "It's too late to be thinking anyway."

Ten minutes later Becky pulled up in front of an apartment block in a newer part of town and sighed lightly as she put her car in gear.

"I remember when all this was wide-open fields." Becky stacked her hands on the steering wheel and rested her chin on them. "That's the trouble with time. It moves and changes things."

"You'd sooner things stay the same."

Becky gave a light shrug. "I'm sentimental. I'll admit it." She turned to Rick, who was sitting slightly askew in his seat watching her. The streetlights above put his face in intriguing shadows, creating a soft intimacy. "Bad habit."

"It can cause a lot of disappointment." He tilted his

head to one side, his slow smile shifting his expression. "But you seem like a person who can rise above it."

"I try. I don't always succeed. I'm only human."

"And now you've got me to deal with."

"It's been an interesting ride, I'll say," she said carefully.

Rick's smile grew. "Diplomatic of you. But speaking of ride, I need to finalize plans for the trail ride. I've got the information in my apartment. Do you have a few moments to come up?"

Fifteen minutes ago Becky had been bone weary, wanting nothing more than home, a hot bath and a cup of hot chocolate. Surprisingly enough, she didn't feel that tired anymore.

"Sure." She turned off the engine and slipped out the door into the cool night air, following Rick up the walk and into the building.

Rick unlocked the door of his apartment and let her in.

"The apartment came furnished, so I can't take any credit or blame for how it looks," he said as he stood aside to let her in.

"It looks fine," Becky said, taking in the minimal furniture, the complete lack of any personal touches. It was just like his office. No photographs, no paintings, posters or anything that expressed who he was.

Sort of like his Day-Timer.

Becky couldn't help but think of her own room and her hotchpotch decorating style. Fans and kites and plants and bowls and cloths hung on walls or were scattered wherever she saw a bare spot that needed a little cheering up. And pictures—family members, friends, fellow workers, people from church, her youth group— all tacked in glorious disarray on a huge bulletin board.

Rick pulled a folder out of a desk drawer and laid it on the table. "I've got all the information right here. Dates of departure and arrival. Also, a general idea of what Triple Bar J is looking for in terms of coverage."

"Wow. A file folder for a trail ride." She quashed a smile at own her flippant comment.

"Okay, enough about my personal management style. It works for me." Rick gave her a crooked grin and she felt a moment of accord. "So, will you be able to go?"

"Not sure yet. Things aren't looking really great."

"Try. I'd like you to come." He held her gaze, his expression softening.

"Okay."

"Do you want a cup of coffee or something like that? Believe it or not, I actually have stuff like that in my house. Cookies, too."

Her first instinct was to say no, she didn't really have time. But the very bareness of his kitchen, the starkness of the rest of the apartment made her relent. She doubted he had much of a social life apart from work.

"That'd be nice. If you have tea, I'd love a cup. I'm not much of a coffee drinker."

"Tea, it is. Flavored, herbal or regular?"

"Wow. A choice." She laughed. "Surprise me."

"I'll try." As he got up, Rick flashed her another grin and Becky felt another flicker of response.

A few moments later he brought out a tray holding a pot of tea, two mugs and a plate of cookies. He cleared a space among the papers and set it down.

"Very domesticated," Becky said, taking the cup he handed her. "I confess I wouldn't have been surprised if you brought out instant coffee in tin cans."

"A habit I picked up. Grandpa was a tea connoisseur." Rick set the plate of cookies in front of her. "The boarding school I went to served tea at night. British roots I suspect. When I traveled I found the tea to be more dependable than the coffee."

"Did you like boarding school?"

"Not particularly, but I never knew different. When Mom died, boarding school was the best alternative for Grandpa Colson." That his words were delivered without any emotion tugged at the motherly part of Becky's heart. She pictured a lost little boy of seven, heading off to a strange place, all alone.

"Did he miss you?"

Rick's laugh was without humor. "I think he waved me off each Monday with a huge sigh of relief."

"I understand Grandpa Colson once made my own grandmother's heart go pit-a-pat. Do you have any pictures of him?"

"No. He wasn't big on photos."

"Must be genetic." Becky glanced around his bare apartment walls. "I kind of thought a photographer would at least have some pictures on the wall."

"Most of my stuff is in boxes. I never stayed in one place long enough to hang things up."

He stated the information casually, but Becky sensed a touch of melancholy in his voice. Or maybe her own sentimental nature imagined it.

"So not even a photo album?"

"I have one I've compiled of trips I've made that I usually take with me in case I want to add to it."

"Can I see it?"

Rick held her gaze as if trying to see past her question. Then with a light shrug, he pushed himself back from the table, got up and walked over to a box that sat beside his couch.

"If it's too much trouble..." Becky suddenly felt as if she were snooping.

"No. It's right here." Rick crouched down and flipped through the box's contents and pulled out a small worn album. He brushed the cover before he handed it to Becky.

Becky opened it up to a picture of an older man sketching a giggling young girl and her solemn older brother. "Where is this?"

"Paris. Montmartre. A bit cliché, but it was my first trip." Rick stayed beside her, his one hand leaning on the table beside the book as Becky turned the pages. His suit coat hung open and his closeness created a curious mixture of discomfort and allure.

"That next one is Mathematician's Square close to Sorbonne."

"No Eiffel Tower?" Becky teased, hoping to find a balance to her seesawing emotions.

"I was trying already then to establish myself as an individual," Rick said with a light laugh. He pulled a chair close and sat down beside her, and allure, for the moment, won.

The pictures changed in composition as she went. From traditional camera angles and European settings, Rick had moved to more far-flung locations, experimenting with light and color as he went. A few striking shots taken in Africa were in black and white, others in sepia tones. Children and families featured in many of the shots.

"I knew you traveled a lot. I never realized how much." As Becky turned the pages, she felt as if she was transported to other, exotic worlds.

"Have you ever traveled?"

Becky shook her head as she turned the page to a picture of a crowded, narrow street. "I've never had the opportunity."

"You don't have opportunities, you take them."

Which sounded suspiciously like his comment about finding time to write. "Maybe someday. I have to confess, though, it seems like a waste of money."

"Traveling isn't something selfish. It can have a purpose."

Becky glanced sidelong at him intrigued by his comment, but he was looking at the album. "And what was your purpose?"

Rick shrugged, glancing up at her. "My articles." He got up and walked around to where he was sitting before, and Becky wondered if she had scared him away. "I made good money doing them. Showing people like you, who don't like to travel, what the world is like."

"I didn't say I don't like to travel." As she closed the album, she noticed a picture tucked away at the back.

It was of a woman holding a young boy on her lap, both of them laughing up at the camera. Becky stopped and looked at it more closely. "Is this you?"

"And my mother."

"Did your dad take it?"

Rick shook his head, toying with his mug. "She always told me a friend took them. I didn't know my father."

"I'm sorry to hear that," Becky said softly.

Rick's sent a curious smile her way. "You don't have to pity me. There are many people in this world who haven't had a third of what I've had."

"Not pity, but I feel bad that you have so few relationships in your life."

A veil dropped over Rick's expression. "I believe you mean that."

Becky couldn't look away and found she didn't want to. As their eyes held, she could almost feel a softening in him. "I do. People shouldn't be alone."

Rick blinked, then a peculiar look drifted over his face. "I'm not alone now." His voice had grown quiet, deeper, and he leaned a little closer, his index finger lightly caressing her hand.

"That sounds an awful lot like a pickup line, Rick," Becky said, hoping she sounded more nonchalant than she felt. In spite of her brief annoyance at his convenient sidestep into insincere patter, she couldn't stop a responding frisson of attraction at his touch.

Rick slipped his fingers inside the palm of her hand as he shrugged. "It probably is."

"So why did you use it? Was I getting too close?"

"Did you take psychology as well as journalism?" he asked, still holding her hand, his eyes concentrating on her fingers.

"No. I think I know you and your kind."

"Ah, a woman of the world in spite of her Christian upbringing." He smiled, but Becky could sense it was forced.

"Christian doesn't mean naive," she said sharply. "I have had a few boyfriends."

"Past tense I notice."

Becky pulled her hand out of his, retreating to the distance she shouldn't have crossed. "I thought I came up here to get some information from you."

"And all you got so far was a cup of tea and confessions."

Rick's comment reminded her that she had stepped out of the boundaries of their relationship as well as he had. He looked at her again, but this time his expression was serious. "I can give it to you on Monday" was all he said.

He wanted her to leave and suddenly she didn't want to go. "I'm here now. I may as well get it."

With a light shrug of resignation, Rick opened the file and pulled out a couple of pieces of paper. He slipped them across the table to her, but didn't meet her eyes. "Even though we're only going two days, the people at Triple Bar J wanted to make things as easy as possible for us, so they gave me some background information." He pulled out another single sheet of paper. "This is what we'll be doing and a list of personal items you need to take if you come. They'll be packing it in on horses so they have a maximum weight you're allowed."

Becky glanced over the list. "I hope I can find the time to go."

"I hope so, too."

His quiet response was far more sincere than his previous one, which made Becky look up at him, faint surprise drifting through her.

Rick didn't look away immediately, and once again Becky felt the same arc of awareness she had felt the first time she met him.

Please, Lord, I can't be attracted to him. He's not the man for me.

But at the same time she didn't want to look away.

"So, what're you guys tryin' to prove?" Katherine Dubowsky didn't quite slam Becky's breakfast on the table, but if the silverware hadn't been lying on a napkin, it would have rattled.

"'Guys'? 'Prove'?" As if Becky didn't know what made Katherine glare down at her, Katherine's penciled-in eyebrows yanked down over her dark eyes in a sharp V.

Most likely the same thing that had made the usual coffee shop conversation die down the moment Becky stepped into Coffee's On.

"Makin' us sound like we don't know how to run a business." Katherine leaned on the table, bringing her angry face closer to Becky's. "That Gavin. Acts like he's the big shot around town. Like his own business is running so peachy keen. Which it ain't."

Becky glanced around the coffee shop. A few of the patrons were avidly watching the exchange, others were looking intently at their food. But Becky knew they were listening just as hard.

She had Rick to thank for putting her in this tricky situation. "It's a column we're trying out for now. If it doesn't work, well, then it doesn't work."

"Well, let me tell you, hon. It doesn't work." Katherine pushed herself away from the table. "Though I sure had to laugh at that 'Runaround Sue' piece."

"And what did you think of the rest of the magazine?" Kim waggled her hand as if balancing the pros and cons. "It looks nice. Lots of ads though. I liked the cowboy article in the 'People and Places' part. Sometimes those pieces could be kind of smarmy. But this one I liked."

Smarmy. Becky squirmed at the word. She had written most of those pieces in the past. That this one, the one that Katherine liked the best, had been done with Rick's help, galled a little.

"Ya gotta lose that Gavin guy," Earl McCrae, a feedlot owner sitting at the next table piped in. He adjusted the dusty cap on his head. "He's trouble."

"Thanks, Earl. I'll make note of it." At least the "trouble" comment balanced out the "smarmy" comment. So far, she and Rick were even.

Katherine tapped her index finger twice on Becky's table as if underscoring Earl's words. "Enjoy your breakfast" was all she said.

As if that was going to happen.

Becky had ducked into Coffee's On early this morning with her notebook computer and the faint hope that she could get a bit of work done on her book. But the atmosphere in the coffee shop was hardly conducive to the writing she'd hoped to do. She pushed it aside, and made short work of her toast and tea.

Chapter Seven

"Any positive letters from the column in the bunch?" Rick leaned back in his chair, his arms crossed over his chest. The early-morning sun gilded his hair and enhanced the smooth cast of his features. In spite of her momentary pique with him over her confrontation with Katherine, Becky couldn't stop the faint lift of her heart.

Okay, he was good-looking and she was a normal woman. A lonely, normal woman. Get on with what you came here for.

"Gavin's sister sent a very encouraging e-mail," Becky continued, willing to concede only this small point.

Trixie had sorted through the mail and stacked all the letters responding to Gavin's article. Compared to the amount of mail the magazine usually generated, this was a glut.

Becky resisted the urge to gloat. Even smile. Being right was enough reward for her. Even so, she couldn't stop her foot from swinging just a bit.

"The language in the letters is pretty strong."

"Not as strong as Gavin's column was."

Rick tapped his thumb against his chin. "I'm not ready to give up on him."

"I had a lovely conversation with Katherine Dubowsky only a few moments ago at Coffee's On. Not impressed. Neither were about half of the customers." She kept Katherine's comment about the cowboy article to herself. Rick didn't need any more ammunition.

"Coffee shop complaints."

"Well, they're complaining about Gavin. And on top of these letters, I'm listening. I have to live in this place, Rick, and with the repercussions."

"I still think they'll get used to him."

Goodness, the man was stubborn.

Becky reached across Rick's desk and flipped through a few envelopes, saving her best shot for last. "I believe here's one from a business called Clip 'n Curl that didn't appreciate some of Gavin's comments."

"That's a hairdresser."

Becky tapped it lightly on the desk. "Not just any hairdresser. Lanette, the owner, calls the owner of Triple Bar J Daddy." Becky shrugged, trying not to enjoy the moment too much. "I don't know which you want to sacrifice—Gavin or..." Becky let the question hang and added a light shrug for emphasis.

Rick rocked in his chair. Then he stopped, as if ready to concede. "You're enjoying this, aren't you?" he said finally, a grin teasing his mouth. "The downfall of the Easterner."

Becky opened her mouth to refute his statement and caught the twinkle in his eye. "Okay. I'll admit it. I love being right."

"If I drop Gavin I'll have to come up with something

short for that space." Rick came around to the front of the desk as if to confront her face-to-face. But Becky knew he was giving in and didn't feel threatened by his nearness.

Felt something else, but she didn't want to examine that too closely.

A month ago Becky would have recommended they bring Gladys back, but even one issue in, Becky knew Gladys wouldn't fit anymore. "Do you want me to find someone?"

"No. I'll take care of it."

She didn't have time to enjoy her victory and launched herself out of her chair. "I gotta run. I'm covering the grand opening of the new car dealership. We promised the owner some good coverage."

"I understand the member of the legislative assembly might be there."

"He better show up. He's a brother-in-law of the owner."

"How do you know all this stuff?" Rick sounded surprised.

"I've lived in this community all my life, Rick. In spite of the many changes that have happened here, I know most of the connections and relationships."

"And that's how you knew Gavin's column wouldn't fly. That kind of intuition works for Okotoks, I'll grant you that much, but when the magazine expands its influence..."

"I still don't think a column like Gavin's works. He's far too negative. I would guess, as a rule, people don't like being told in polysyllabic words that they are dolts who don't know how to run their business."

"I still think he had some good advice."

Becky knew she should stop. Her point had been made. She had been proved right. But she couldn't. Something about Rick's comments, his attitude, created an unreasoning need to bring up a contrary view. "It wasn't his advice, Rick. It was his presentation."

"So he should have wrapped it up in pretty words."

Gracious, he was as bad as she was. "Didn't you ever have to take bad medicine?" she asked. "Didn't your mother ever put some sugar in it to make it easier to go down? Deceitful, yes, but if you're doing what you're doing out of concern, then by all means, use a little bit of sugar."

"We're not dealing with kids. Anyone who has any kind of business has had to deal with problems and setbacks. Don't tell me they don't know how to take bad news." Rick dropped one hip against his desk and crossed his arms.

Becky glanced at the clock on Rick's wall. She didn't have time to argue but she couldn't seem to stop. "You agree that he was a mistake. Why replow this old ground?" Becky couldn't keep the exasperation out of her voice.

Now Rick swung his foot, his dimple deepening in one cheek as he gave her an engaging smile. "Maybe I like arguing with you. And maybe I want to show you that even though you were right, I was a little bit right, too."

The teasing tone of his voice coupled with his charming smile brought out a responding grin. "Okay. You were right, too. Hard news for hard times." She stopped the "but" that was forming and let it lie.

"So are you going to allow me the last word?"

Anything she said right now would be self-fulfilling, so she simply nodded.

"Great. That's all I wanted." He reached over and patted her on the shoulder. "Go and enjoy the grand opening."

His gesture was almost fatherly, but the feelings it aroused in her were hardly those of a daughter. And as their eyes met again she felt herself drawn once again to him, like a moth to a flame.

Dangerous.

She left as quickly as she could.

We've got more trained accountants in the government's Treasury Department than a politician has promises, and all have the imagination of plywood. My idea of an ideal treasurer would be a mother of four children, married to a wage earner—someone who has learned to make do— to manage a budget that doesn't change with every whim. Imagine the meetings. "Madame Treasurer, I would like to request funding for an arts project that seeks to discover the self-actualization of dirt within a cultural concept." Once she's picked herself up from the floor and wiped the tears of laughter from her eyes, I'm sure they will have received their answer...

Runaround Sue

If only life were as simple as Runaround Sue would imagine it to be. I wonder what her hypothetical mother of four children would do when asked to respond to the issue of deregulation of the power industry. Not as easy as handing out chore lists. But it's something that local businesses have

had to deal with and must continue to face. This
is a hard world full of bad news....

Becky smiled when she read Rick's column. He had
asked to see what Runaround Sue had written before he
wrote up his and this was the result. Not all-out war, but
the battle lines were getting drawn. A gentle tug of the
gloves.

Well, Sue was up to the challenge, Becky thought,
already planning her next column. She just wished her
book were as easy to write as the "Runaround Sue" columns were.

"Have a seat, Rick, and tell me what your grandfather has been up to lately," Diene De Graaf said, patting
the empty spot on the sofa beside her. Rick sat down,
glancing around Sam and Cora's living room as he did.
Becky sat, legs crossed on the floor across the room,
playing a board game with her nieces and nephew. She
wore her hair up today, arranged in some combination
of curls and pins that looked cute on her. Her hazel eyes
sparkled as she cheered on her nephew.

"My grandfather is busy building up his empire,"
Rick said, forcing his attention back to Becky's grandmother. Of all the people he had met in Becky's family,
Diene resembled her most. Same bright eyes that held
a touch of humor. Same slightly stubborn jaw and laughing mouth. "Grandfather has made his mark in Toronto.
Now it seems he wants to do the same in Okotoks."

Diene laughed lightly. "He always was a man of vision. Even when he was living here."

"He never told me he lived here. Or that he knew

you." Rick could see why his grandfather might have, at one time, been attracted to Diene. Age had only smudged her beauty, not diminished it.

Diene sat back in the couch, smiling lightly. "He was quite the gentleman. Just not the kind of man I saw myself having a future with."

A peal of laughter drew Rick's attention to Becky. She was lying flat out on the ground, giggling now, while her nephew and nieces swarmed over her. "You helped him...I saw you...no fair." The accusations flew at her like popcorn, but even Rick could tell they weren't really angry.

Becky sat up and scooped the three kids close to her in a group hug. "I love you all, bumpkins," she said, still giggling. "Now go get me some cake."

As the children scattered, Becky smoothed her hair and tugged her shirt straight. Then she looked up and their gazes tangled and clung.

He didn't imagine her soft smile, nor how it made his own heart skip. Just a little. Rick dragged his attention back to Diene and the comment she had made. "And what kind would that be?"

"The same kind of man Becky has been holding out for. A man who knows the Lord."

Rick didn't have to look at Diene to feel the gentle warning in her words.

He wanted to pass off his attraction to Becky as the simple chemistry he had felt when he first saw her.

However, he knew that time with her had desimplified the attraction. She wasn't just a pretty, young woman. He had come to know her in other ways. Had come to admire her ability to stand up to him. To challenge him. Though he and Becky had never talked much about it, he knew her relationship to God was real and true and positive.

Becky got up and glanced his way, holding his gaze as they caught. Neither looked away.

In that moment Rick felt the subtle shift, a realignment of the relationship.

And from the frown making a number eleven between Diene's eyebrows, Rick could tell that she had felt it, too.

"You know, Rick," she said laying a hand on his arm. "A grandmother is not supposed to have favorites, but Becky has always held a special place in my heart. Of all my children and grandchildren, she is the most like me." She pressed her fingers down, as if warning him. "I never dated any man unless I saw them as a future life partner. Becky is the same. She's not a person to go on casual dates. But the most important reason I turned your grandfather down was because I knew his heart wasn't right with God at the time."

In spite of her words, though, Rick heard the unspoken question threaded through her voice.

"Grandfather Colson goes to church," Rick said. "He raised my mother to fear God. If that means anything."

Diene smiled and Rick caught a glimpse of yearning mixed with sadness. "I'm glad for that," she whispered. "Did he teach you?"

"He tried." Rick held her gaze and once again felt the faint echo of what had touched him in church when Becky sang. But he wasn't going to give in that easily. "What I've seen in the world hasn't endeared me to God."

"How can a loving God allow so much suffering?" she said softly, voicing his thoughts.

"Yes." Her candid question surprised him. "And as long as I'm asking those kind of questions, I can't see that God would be interested in me."

She smiled, looking into the middle distance as if seeking her answer there. "Your grandfather often asked the same question. Interesting that you two are that much alike." She turned to face him. "It's a good question to ask, Rick. And God respects the asking. He wants honesty in His relationships with His people. Not fake devotion." She patted him lightly on the arm. "Keep your heart open to God. He's not afraid to be asked the hard questions."

Rick felt a glimmering of truth kindle in him as he held Diene's eyes. And what other questions would God be able to handle?

"Hey, Mother. Find out all the things you wanted to about your old honey?" Becky's father dropped onto the couch on the other side of Diene and winked at Rick. The moment was broken.

"Mother used to have quite a thing for your grandfather," Sam said in a hearty voice. "And now I've made her blush."

Diene tutted lightly, shaking her head. "If you don't have anything constructive to say, I'm leaving."

"My mother's a good woman," Sam said, laughing as Diene strode to the kitchen. "Just doesn't take to teasing. Did you want to see the rest of the orchard?"

What Rick wanted was to see Becky again, but she was nowhere in sight.

Colette grabbed her sister by the arm, dragging her up the stairs by the kitchen. "Becks, this Rick is adorable," Colette said in a stage whisper, glancing over her shoulder.

"That's exactly what Leanne said. Do you girls subscribe to the same magazines?" Becky laughed off her sister's gushing comment.

"Have your little joke. I see the way you two look at each other." Colette winked at her sister. "Just like me and Nick." Colette pulled her down on the stairs, her knees drawn up to her chin. "Now, tell me more about him. Leanne said he was good-looking, but the words don't do him justice."

Becky sighed, indulging in her younger sister's high school–style gossipfest. She knew she would have no rest until she set the record straight.

"Rick is single. Comes from Toronto originally. He's Colson Ethier's grandson and is here to bring *Going West* into the next century. He likes to travel and drinks tea. I believe he's about six feet tall. Would have to guess on the weight." Becky ticked the items off on her fingers aware of Colette's growing impatience.

Colette pushed Becky's hand down. "Very funny. Now tell me what I really want to know."

Becky sighed and inspected her fingernails. Saw a hangnail.

"Don't even think about it." Colette stopped Becky's hand halfway up to her mouth. "So. Tell me."

"Honestly, Colette. There's nothing to say. He's only here for a little bit and then he'll be gone. And I'm too busy."

"You're always too busy. You should drop a few things."

"Like what? The minister was campaigning for about three weeks to get someone to do kids' choir. I can't leave the library board until they find a replacement for me. The worship committee can never find enough volunteers. Sandy needs me to help her with the youth..." Becky laced her fingers together. "And I'm trying to find time to write my book."

Colette put her hand on her sister's shoulder and gave her a light shake. "Your problem is you're too good at the things you do."

"Well, I feel that God has given me gifts I need to use. And I feel that I'm serving Him by using them in our church."

"But surely you don't have to use them all at once."

Becky laughed. "Well, for now, this is my life and I'm happy with it."

"Just too busy to do anything about your good-lookin' boss."

"And may I remind you, he is my boss."

Colette groaned.

"C'mon. Let's see if we can use our dishwashing talents and help our mother out." Becky jumped off the stairs and held out her hand to her sister.

"But you have to admit, he is a hunk."

And Colette didn't need to know that there were times that Becky would agree with that statement.

"I should cut down those old trees, but I hate to do it." Sam stood in front of a particularly gnarled tree. "Cora's grandfather started these."

Rick thought of his grandfather's current home. Colson had bought it three years ago. It, too, had stately trees and a well-landscaped yard but he knew nothing about it. Nor cared.

But Sam knew every tree in his extensive orchard as if by name. A heritage, he thought with a faint touch of envy.

The sound of a motor drew nearer and then they heard "Hey, Dad" above its intrusive snarl.

Rick spun around, his heart lifting when he saw Becky astride an ATV heading toward them. She stopped in front of them and vaulted off, slightly breathless, her cheeks flushed, her eyes bright.

"That guy you needed to get a hold of in Holland just called."

"Is he still on the phone?"

"Take the quad. He said he'd wait." Becky's eyes were on her father, but Rick felt a tug of connection.

"Thanks, sweetie. I'll see you two back at the house." He dropped a light kiss on Becky's head, jumped aboard the four-wheeler, spun it around and left in a cloud of exhaust and noise.

Becky turned to him. "Sorry about Dad dragging you out here. He gets a little obsessed about his orchard at times. Show the least bit of interest and you're his next victim."

"He was just showing me this apple tree." Rick pointed to the old tree beside him. "Telling me the history."

"The Opa tree?" Becky smiled as she reached up to grab a rough, crooked branch, its leaves rustling as she shook it lightly. "I remember getting material for budding off it in the summer and apples in the fall. Poor tree. We used and abused it."

"He told me your great-grandfather planted it."

"Actually, he planted the rootstock. Only native or wild apple trees can overwinter in this climate, but they produce small hard inedible apples. These branches were grafted onto the wild rootstock and produce large, tasty apples. So the wild and the tame work together and need each other. It's an old tree." Becky gave the branch another shake, looking up through the leaves, her head thrown back. "It got struck by lightning once. You can see up there, at the top. It's still the biggest tree in the orchard though."

Rick wasn't looking at the tree though, his eyes fixed on Becky.

"Obviously a lot of memories here." He shouldn't feel the faint tug of envy he did at her history. He never had any desire to be so rooted.

Becky angled him a quick smile as she walked around the tree. "We used to hide in it, though if Opa ever caught us, we'd be weeding the new orchard by hand. Mostly we don't let the trees get this big. Makes it too hard to pick the apples. But this one is special and we don't prune it anymore."

"You still work in the orchard?" Rick followed her around the tree, lured on by the smile she had given him. Something had shifted between them in the past few days and he wanted to explore it.

"I try to. Just too busy these days."

"I know. I didn't think you could fit anything more in that Day-Timer of yours."

Becky's horrified look came at the same instant he realized what he had said.

"I'm sorry," he muttered, holding his hand up in a gesture of surrender. "I just... When I had it, I opened it up because I thought it was mine."

To his surprise Becky didn't get angry. Didn't ask what he was doing snooping through her book. Instead she stared at the tree, her hands still holding on to a lower branch.

"It was an honest mistake," he continued, trying to catch her eye.

"How much did you see?" she asked quietly, licking her lips.

"I saw that every available moment of every available day is full," he answered, evading her question neatly. "I also saw that you're going to have to do some major rescheduling if you're going to go on the trail ride."

Becky caught one corner of her lip between her teeth. "About that ride..."

"You're not going to beg off on me, are you?" His reasons for wanting her to come were mixed. He wasn't sure himself. Only that the more he thought of spending some time with her away from the office, the more he liked the idea.

"No. It's just that—" she lifted her hands as if in a gesture of surrender "—I have a lot of obligations."

"And a financial obligation to the magazine."

"That's true."

He sensed she was wavering and pushed his advantage. "I'm going to need your perspective. Otherwise all I might write about is the mess the horses leave behind and how cold it is in the mountains."

Becky laughed. "Okay. I'll see what I can do." She picked at a hangnail, still looking down. "So, what else did you see in my Day-Timer?"

He could be evasive and keep her secret, or he could be honest and maybe find out if her feelings had changed. "I did read that you weren't quite sure what to do about me."

Becky closed her eyes and blew out her breath. "I'm sorry," she said quietly. "I was worried about working with you. And maybe a little angry with you yet over my book review." Becky glanced up at him, her expression serious now. "I poured my heart and soul into that book. Though I should have felt honored that you read it, it was still hard to see it trashed so publicly."

Guilt twanged through Rick. "My grandfather wasn't happy with how I'd handled it, either. After the review came out in the magazine I found out that he hadn't given me the book to review. He had been hoping it would touch some cold part of my heart."

Becky gave him a wry smile, which surprised him and encouraged him at the same time. "Guess I failed in that, too."

"Not completely. There were some genuinely moving pieces and I did finish the book."

"I know you well enough to know there's a huge 'but' hanging here." She winced. "If you'll forgive how that sounded."

Rick couldn't stop his laugh. Couldn't stop himself from taking a step closer to her, encouraged by her honesty. "Okay. The but." He paused, trying to find the right words. "I don't think this story was the right vehicle for what you wanted to say. It was melodramatic. Too derivative of many books out there. Once in a while you had a passage that rose above the rest of the book, but then you seemed to pull your writing down to make it fit the story."

She held his gaze, her head canted to one side. Smiled a bit. And his heartbeat fluttered a moment.

"Okay, I'll concede that," she said. "How could I

have done it differently?" She came around the tree, took a step closer to him, one hand still holding on to the trunk as if seeking strength from her great-grandfather's legacy.

"You need to take more time with your story. Commit emotionally to the book. Put yourself in it."

"Funny. I thought I had done that."

"Not really. You're a funnier person than the story shows. A more optimistic person. I think you might benefit from writing a story in first person. Getting deeper into the character. Being more honest. Exposing yourself."

"Hey! I'm a good Christian girl," Becky said with a laugh, hitting him lightly on the chest.

Before he could stop to think what he was doing, Rick captured her hand against his chest, captivated himself by her honest humor. He held her hand close, its warmth pressing through his shirt.

Becky's gaze jumped to his face, her eyes searching his features as if trying to discover what he wanted, what had changed between them. She swallowed, then let her gaze fall to their joined hands as she pressed her fingers ever so lightly against his shirt.

Rick curled his fingers around hers, wondering if she could feel the increased tempo of his own heart.

"I should go help—help my mom," Becky whispered. But even as she spoke, she took a slow step closer.

"I think your mom can manage." Rick rubbed his thumb along the back of her hand, wondering what his next step was.

He didn't usually have to second-guess himself. A

hand under her chin. A careful, encouraging smile. Then the kiss. All carefully choreographed and planned.

But he didn't want to treat her like other women. She was special. He wanted to share more than a kiss. More than the physical expression of love. But she was a sincere Christian who loved her Lord. And he didn't know if he could share that with her.

Becky looked up at him then and he saw his own confusion mirrored in her soft hazel eyes. "What's happening, Rick?" she whispered.

He gently fingered a tendril of hair back behind her ear, his hand lingering on her neck as a stillness surrounded them. As if the very trees waited, wondering what they were going to do. "Come on the trail ride. Maybe we can find out more."

"I'll try."

A muffled giggle slipped into the silence followed by the soft "plop" of an apple in the grass at their feet.

Becky blinked, as if coming out of a trance, then pulled her hand away, turning to the source of the laughter.

"Okay, you brats. You can come out now," she said loudly. But Rick heard the faint tremor in her voice and was encouraged. She had been as moved as he had.

The three children Becky had been playing with spilled out from behind a row of bushes, followed by Leanne.

"We were wondering where you were," Leanne said, tossing a speculative glance Rick's way. "Grandma Diene sent us to get you."

More likely, protect you, Rick thought, remembering Diene De Graaf's veiled warning.

The children ran to Becky, but the smallest girl

veered at the last moment and lifted her arms up to Rick. "You carry me," she said with a child's brashness.

"Serena, be polite," Becky reprimanded. "Maybe Mr. Ethier doesn't want to carry you."

"Please carry me," Serena said, adding an angelic smile.

"Of course." Rick swung her up onto his shoulders as she squealed her appreciation. "You have to duck for the trees," he warned as he glanced sidelong at Becky.

She stood in front of him, bracketed by a boy and a girl, a faint smile teasing her lips as a breeze teased her hair. Rick winked at her—a casual connection to ease themselves away from the intimacy of the previous moment—then turned and sauntered back to the house.

But even though his long legs easily outpaced Becky, he was less aware of the little girl on his shoulder, clutching his head, than he was of Becky walking behind him.

Chapter Eight

Rick looked over the parking lot of the church full of minivans, cars with children's car seats, sports cars and trucks. All representing a family, a person, a couple inside. And singing, from the sounds that streamed through the door beside him.

Since that Sunday when Becky had finessed him into coming to church, he hadn't found—or made—time to attend. Yet each Sunday, when he passed the building, he had wondered if he would find something behind those doors. The same nebulous something that had called to him that Sunday when Becky sang the prayer.

So who was he interested in? God? Becky? Both?

He took a hesitant step toward the door. Then, releasing a sigh, he pulled the door open and stepped inside. The sounds of the singing drew him on and he slipped through the narthex into the sanctuary. The congregation was standing, but thankfully there was an empty space at the end of the back pew and he took his place in it and let the music and the words take him along.

And then he saw her.

Becky stood in the front of the church, with a group of young children lined up in three rows. She had her back to the congregation, but from where he sat Rick could see her face in profile as she and the children sang along with the congregation. She wore the same blue dress she had the first Sunday he'd seen her. And she looked just as beautiful as she had then. Maybe even more so.

Then the song ended, the congregation sat down and Becky turned around to address them.

"I'm sure many of you parents have been wondering what your children have been doing all those Wednesday nights when they disappear with me to one of the downstairs rooms," she said, looking around the sanctuary. "Well, this morning you're going to get a sample of the program the choir is putting on tonight. Think of it as a teaser. And if that's not enough to tempt you to come tonight, then I feel I should mention that the Ladies' Aid Society is hosting a dessert night in conjunction with the program. So if you want a taste of Gladys Hemple's chocolate cake..." Becky raised her hands in a "what can I do?" gesture. Then with a smile, she turned around, cued the musicians, lifted her hands with a smile to the children and they began.

The song was a light, happy tune, an introduction to the story of Jonah and the whale. Becky's animated expression was contagious and the children responded with wide smiles.

Their light voices were clear and boisterous as they sang about a reluctant prophet who questioned God and who God used anyway. Rick caught himself humming along during the chorus, smiling at the children's obvious enjoyment.

When they were done, Becky nodded, and with a surprising amount of restraint the children walked back to their parents, grinning with pride.

Becky stayed in the front and when the regular worship team came up, she ducked out a side door.

Probably off to perform yet another obligation, Rick thought. And for a moment he was tempted to leave, as well, but the minister came forward. It wouldn't look good to leave during the main attraction, Rick thought. So he sat back and settled in for another sermon.

The minister instructed the congregation to open their Bibles to Psalm One and Rick read about a man who does not stand in the counsel of the wicked, but whose delight was in the law. Rick tried to imagine someone who would delight in laws. And rules.

"He is like a tree planted by streams of water which yields its fruit in season and whose leaf does not wither."

Like the trees of Sam Ellison's orchard.

Like Becky. Rooted and grounded. A part of something larger than herself. Her family. This church. Her community.

So what did that make him? The chaff? Blown about with every changing wind. He knew he didn't have what she had.

But did he want it?

"So how do you propose to do this?" Rick's office chair creaked in protest as he leaned way back. He ran his index finger back and forth over his forehead as if trying to draw some inspiration from his mind. He had been talking to Terry Anderson, their accounts manager at the bank, for twenty minutes now. They still couldn't agree on how to deal with the serious cash-flow problems the magazine was having.

"The magazine needs to show some kind of profit," Terry was saying. "Or at the minimum, break even. At least on the books. The higher-ups are getting a little antsy."

"Waiting for *Going West* to show a profit is like trying to turn the *Titanic*. It doesn't happen in three issues."

"*Going West* hasn't shown a profit for more than three issues, Rick."

Rick turned his chair around so he could at least see the mountains. "This is what you can do for me, Terry. Make it clear to the suits in Calgary that *Going West* has been bought and is under new management. That you foresee a change in the near future. That has to count for something. That to pull the loan now would be a short-term loss and if they wait, they'll have a valuable asset on their hands." Brave words, but it was the only thing he could give Terry right now. "Your job is to go to bat for me, Terry. Once things start looking better, this will reflect well on you."

"My job is also to keep my job."

Rick sighed. "If you pull the loan and you guys end up with a dead asset, your job won't be looking that good, either, Terry."

The silence on the other end meant Terry was considering and Rick pushed a little harder. "We've got a dynamite issue coming up, Terry. Surely the bank won't go belly-up by extending our line of credit for another six weeks."

"I'll see what I can do," Terry said. "I'll let you know which way the wind blows as soon after our next meeting. I think I've made it clear that *Going West* is in a precarious position."

"Whatever. And while I have you on the phone, would the bank consider putting an ad in the next magazine?"

"You don't quit, do you?"

"And that's exactly what is going to make the difference in the long run." Rick grinned as relief sluiced through him. In spite of Terry's warning, he knew he had bought some time.

He rang off and picked up the latest issue of the magazine. He turned the page, pleased with the overall result of this, his second magazine. It looked professional. The content needed a little boost, but that was coming, as well. He and Becky didn't always agree on what to put in, but slowly they were coming to a compromise that seemed to work.

He turned to the page that held his and Sue's column.

I think it's time newspapers own up to the old adage Bad News Travels By Itself and not help the business along. For once I'd like to read how millions of children got tucked into bed last night. Millions of married couples didn't have a fight or threaten to kill each other. Millions of people made it home safely from work. Millions of people did their jobs well today. "This is not news," the newsmakers wail, gripping their foam-covered microphones and waiting for a disaster to backlight their perfectly coiffed hair....

Runaround Sue

The most important task of any magazine, news-paper or newscast is the delivery of timely and per-tinent information according to its subscribers needs and wants. Sue clearly states that bad news travels by itself, but it is the bad news that often determines how businessmen will make their decisions....

Rick couldn't help but smile. He'd never admit it aloud, and especially not to Becky, but Sue had a point. He wouldn't mind meeting her; she sounded like an in-teresting person.

Someone knocked lightly on the door and Becky stuck her head inside his office. "Hey, there. You busy? Trixie said you were on the phone."

"No. Come on in."

Becky shook her head. "I gotta run. Just thought I'd tell you that I will be able to go on the trail ride with you. I cleared a few things off my calendar, so—" she tossed her head a bit as if mentally juggling her new schedule "—let me know when you want to leave."

"That's great, Becky." His first good news of the day.

She retreated with a quick smile.

And Rick started planning.

Becky leaned forward, as if to catch a better view of the purple-tinted mountains rising and rising out of the prairies, dominating the horizon. They rimmed the sky, jagged and awe-inspiring, their snow-covered peaks blindingly white against a sapphire sky.

The road Becky traveled on wound through rolling foothills, wooded with pines, but the mountains stood sentinel, exerting an inexorable pull, daring any to look away. It had been a while since she'd seen the mountains this close and she couldn't look away. Thankfully the road leading to the ranch was quiet, or she might have run the risk of an accident.

An arch holding the Triple Bar J brand came into view. Becky turned and followed the gravel road to the yard she saw nestled in a hollow of a hill.

She pulled up in front of one of many log buildings, hoping it was the horse barn Rick had told her about last night when he phoned to make final preparations.

The phone call had been short. Becky held her questions back. Last night her very helpful sisters had let her know that Rick had been in church Sunday morning. The knowledge had been enough to lift her heart and kindle the faint hope she'd been nurturing since he'd held her hand in her father's orchard.

That moment hadn't been a turning point for her as much as a culmination of the attraction she had felt for him from the moment she saw him. She had tried to dismiss it as a mere physical draw of any woman to a man possessed of Rick's charm.

But she couldn't dismiss the connection she had felt with him then, and, it seemed, anytime they spoke or sparred. That he had come to church added another dimension to that connection.

Where would it go?

Becky got out of the car, shading her eyes against the morning sun as she looked around the yard. A bunch of horses stood patiently waiting in a corral off the horse barn, tails swishing at flies. The more impatient ones shuffled around raising dust that caught in Becky's throat. One horse lifted its head and looked beyond her, its ears pricked forward. Becky turned to see where it was looking.

And why did her heart give one long slow thump then begin racing faster than her car engine on high idle? All it took was the single glimpse of a thin trail of dust coming far down the road, one that could only be from Rick's Jeep, for her involuntary muscle to act even more involuntarily.

"Hey, Becky."

Becky spun around at the voice. The man coming toward her looked as if he had just stepped out of a Western. Tall, lanky, his face shaded from the bright sun by a large cowboy hat, his shirt dusty and sweat stained, his hands encased in leather gloves. The leather chaps swinging around his legs almost covered his slant-heeled boots.

He tugged a glove off his one hand and reached out to her as he tipped his hat back with another, his smile a white slash against his tanned face. His rugged features completed the image of the working cowboy.

"So this is where you ended up, Trevor," Becky said with a nod of recognition. "I should have figured that out."

"If you would have returned my phone calls you would have found out sooner that I was the newly appointed manager of the Triple Bar J." Trevor grinned at her, still holding her hand. "I heard you were coming and made sure I was going to be in charge of the ride."

"When did you start here?"

"A couple of weeks ago. In time to get in on this new thing the boss wanted to do with your magazine." He angled his head to one side, his smile melancholy. "So why didn't you call back?"

At one time, Trevor's interest would have made her heart skip. Now she was more aware of Rick's Jeep pulling up than a former boyfriend who had bruised her heart. "I had nothing to say."

"Well, do you have a smooch for an old boyfriend?" He slipped his arm around her shoulders, but Becky turned her head to one side.

"You can have a hug, but forget the kiss."

"I thought you might at least write me, Becks," he said, bumping her side lightly with his hip. "Didn't you miss me?"

Becky let her gaze tick over his dark hair, chiseled features finally resting on his soft brown eyes. "At first. A bit," she admitted reluctantly.

"But not after a while," he said. Becky shook her head, then turned, her heart giving a quick uptick as Rick closed the door of his vehicle, slung his camera bag over his shoulder and came walking toward them.

He wore a faded denim shirt tucked into equally faded blue jeans and a pair of leather boots that had that soft wrinkled look of steady use. As he sauntered toward them in his loose-hipped walk, Becky's heart started up again.

Trevor easily rivaled Rick in the looks department and Trevor still had his arm across her shoulders. But it was Rick she couldn't keep her eyes off of when he stopped in front of them, pulling his sunglasses off and glancing from Becky to Trevor who held his hand out to Rick.

"You must be Rick Ethier. I'm Trevor Wilson. I'm in charge of the trail ride."

"And a few other things it seems," Rick drawled, and shook Trevor's hand, his eyes flicking over the other arm Trevor still had casually draped across Becky's shoulder.

"Trevor's an old friend," Becky said, surprised at Rick's tone. "Just returned from California via Colorado."

"I tried to convince Becky to come with me when I left, but she turned me down." Trevor gave Becky a one-armed hug. "She's got her roots down deep."

Becky laughed politely, gave Rick a bright smile and pulled herself gently out of Trevor's hold. "Where should I put my things?" she asked Trevor, her eyes noting the absence of Rick's gaze.

"I was told to show you two around the place first. Boss said you wanted to get some pictures of the spread," Trevor said. "The ride isn't scheduled to go out until noon." He grinned at Becky and made to put his arm around her again.

Becky sidestepped and flashed him a warning look. "Lead the way."

Trevor had gathered a lot of information in the short time he had been at the ranch and was a knowledgeable and amiable guide. But Becky made sure to keep her distance.

The ranch had been established at the turn of the century, when the only law was might made right. The original owner was a remittance man, the youngest son of a wealthy family, sent over to the New World because there was no land for him to inherit in England. He was one of the few who had turned his "remittance" from home into land and stock and slowly built up a small empire.

This empire had suffered and prospered through economic ebbs and flows. It was currently owned by a cartel of various businesses, a few with vague connections to ranching and cattle. As Rick snapped pictures, Becky tried to figure how to work the businesses into the article.

An hour and a half later they had worked their way back to the corrals, now a much busier place. People dressed in a variety of Western clothes stood either by their vehicles or by the corrals, watching the horses.

Thankfully Trevor left them to go help saddle up. But Rick followed him, leaving Becky alone and wondering if he had regretted the moment at her parents' place.

Okay. She could be casual, too, if that was how he wanted to play it. She spun on her heel and strode over to chat to a couple she recognized from church. In turn she was introduced to a few more people. Becky was pleased to discover that not all the riders were experienced. It had been a few years since she'd been on a horse, and was a little nervous.

"So I understand that's your new boss." The woman, Nola, angled her chin at Rick. She pushed her white straw cowboy hat off her head, as if to get a better look. "He's a sweetie," she said with a wink at Becky.

Becky glanced over her shoulder at Rick, who was resting his elbows on the corral fence, snapping pictures of the horses. *Sweetie* was not a word she would use with Rick, though at first sight, his poster-boy good looks could be deceiving. "He has his own charm," she conceded.

"Oh, c'mon, Becky. Admit it. He's a looker." Nola gave Becky a quick hug. "I know a dozen young women who would agree. More than a dozen."

Nola's gushing was embarrassing. At the same time it was as if her avid interest in Rick pulled down another of the flimsy barriers Becky had erected against Rick and the very charm Nola was so enthused over.

Yet part of her was annoyed. Rick was so much more

than his looks, and she resented the fact that people saw only that part of him.

"I sure like what he's done with the magazine." Nola tipped her hat back as if to see him better. "He's really made a difference already."

"You don't mind all the ads?"

Nola shrugged. "I don't particularly care for them, and I do kinda miss Edna's corny advice that came with her recipes, but it's a balance, isn't it? I'll tell you what I really like is the way Runaround Sue and Rick are always butting heads. Who is that girl? She's a good writer."

"She's wanting to stay anonymous for now," Becky said vaguely, pleased with Nola's comment. "But I can pass it on."

"Well, you just pass that on to Rick right now. Don't bother spending time with us old folks." Nola gave Becky a push in Rick's direction at the same moment Rick looked over at her. Her momentum carried her toward him. To stop and turn around would have been sillier than to keep going.

Casual and relaxed was called for, though Becky felt anything but.

Weather. That was always a safe topic.

"Trevor figures we won't be seeing much cloud cover," Becky said as she joined him at the fence. "You'll get some nice shots of the Rockies."

"I'm looking forward to that." Rick leaned his elbows on the corral fence, watching the wranglers and the horses, still holding his camera. "So how did you know Trevor?"

"High school fling. I was the editor of the school

newspaper, he was the rodeo king." Becky joined him, stepping up on the first rail so she could see better. "Hardly the classic relationship of cheerleader, football quarterback, but those positions were already taken."

"So the old boyfriend has come back into your life."

Where did this cool tone in his voice come from? Becky tried to catch his gaze, but he was snapping pictures, using the rail as a rest.

"No. Trevor has come back to the Triple Bar J. I'm hardly a concern."

"So that's why you were able to make arrangements suddenly to come on the ride?" Rick asked, with a quick sideways look. "Because Trevor was back?"

If Becky didn't know better, she would have guessed he was jealous. "I didn't know Trevor worked here until I got here."

"You didn't keep up with his comings and goings?"

"Not really," she said. "The dust from his horse trailer had barely settled before I was on to other things."

This wasn't entirely true. She had mooned around the house, listened to Ian Tyson singing "Someday Soon" for months afterward and dreamed about following Trevor on the rodeo circuit. But he never called and Becky grew up and life flowed on, predictable and safe, her heart intact.

"Was there ever anyone else?" Rick asked, his tone casual.

"I've dated a few guys, but Okotoks is hardly the place to meet eligible young men. Most young people want to get out of here as soon as possible."

She wondered at Rick's sudden interest as she rested her chin on her hands watching Trevor sorting the horses. "How about you, Rick? Any old loves in your life?"

"I dated a few girls. Just never stayed in one place long enough to maintain a serious relationship."

A faint chill slivered through her, as if she was being warned. "Maybe you just haven't met the right person," she said carefully, hoping she sounded unconcerned. Then she made the mistake of looking sideways at him. He was looking at her and he wasn't smiling.

"That might be a reason," he said softly.

As she held his gaze, her heart gave a soft flip. And when he turned the camera to her and snapped a couple of pictures, she felt as if he had underlined his comment.

"You can't put those in the article," she said with a light laugh.

"I might find another use for them," he said, winding the film, and stepping off the fence. "We should go pick out our horses."

Half an hour later, Becky and Rick were part of a long column of riders snaking their way along a wooded trail heading up into the mountains. It had taken a bit of maneuvering on Rick's part to get him and Becky to take up the rear together. Fortunately Becky didn't know a lot about horses and Rick did. He'd been checking out the animals and made sure they ended up with passive horses. Now they were exactly where he wanted the two of them to be.

As far away from this Trevor guy as possible.

If it wasn't for the fact that Becky seemed genuinely uninterested in Trevor's obvious come-ons, he might have been more jealous.

Which was a first for him.

The sun was warm on his back, a faint breeze slid over his bared arms. Rick shifted in his saddle, each muffled footfall of the horse on the dirt path, each faint jingle of the horses' tack pushing away the tension that gripped his shoulders and neck. The past couple of weeks had been stressful. On top of getting the art and design team in line with what he wanted the magazine to do, he'd been busy getting potential advertisers aligned with the vision of *Going West,* setting up a budget they could fall within and yet put out a quality magazine.

The worst of his struggles were with the bank. He really shouldn't be going on this trip. He should be trying to get creative about getting the cash flow of the magazine healthy. But when Becky said she was coming on the ride, the cash flow became slightly less of a priority.

Becky turned around in her saddle, her hair loosely tied back, a few strands framing her face. "Isn't this gorgeous?" she said, her smile lighting up her features as she flung her arm to encompass the open space behind them, the trees below them, the mountains rising up. "On days like this, I love my job."

"I thought you loved it all the time?" Rick teased, pulling his horse up beside hers, encouraged by her welcoming smile.

"I do, but honestly, Rick, this is amazing." She shook her head, dropping it back to look up at a sky so blue it hurt. "What a beautiful country we live in."

Her good humor was infectious and Rick couldn't help the smile that started inside and slowly migrated to his face. She rolled her head lightly, looking askance at him. "What do you think?"

Rick reluctantly pulled his gaze away from Becky

and let it flow over the mountains that guarded the valley they were heading up. Rock and snow, folded and bent, pushing up against the sky, overwhelming their tiny column of people, rendering them insignificant. At the same time he felt a sense of peace and protection. Security.

"It's amazing, really. That all this just...is. A picture can't begin to capture the depth and sweep of this valley."

"I lived close to the mountains all my life and I still can't figure out where to look when I look at them. I want to see them all at once, to let their sheer majesty take my breath away, and yet I want to be able to recognize certain parts of them, make them my own." Becky sighed lightly, leaning forward in the saddle. "I haven't come here enough. I'm glad we could do this."

So was he.

They crested a peak, then dropped down into a river valley, the horses ahead of them like a long train, wending its way over the trail.

Rick tied the reins of his horse to the saddle horn and unpacked the camera from the saddlebags. He stopped his horse, and Becky's stopped, as well. He snapped a few pictures of the riders ahead of them. Then, giving in to an impulse, turned and framed Becky against the backdrop of the mountains. Her bright red shirt created a sharp contrast to the azure sky and purple-hazed mountains.

"What are you doing?" She laughed, pushing her windblown hair back from her face. "I told you you're not going to be putting those in the magazine. Conflict of interest and all that."

Ignoring her, he zoomed in on her face. But she

didn't look away. Her hazel eyes looked directly into the camera. The sincerity of her steady gaze and her warm smile slid into his heart. His finger trembled on the shutter as he took another picture, stored another memory on film.

"We should get going," Becky said as he lowered his camera, shaken by the innocent encounter. "We're going to fall behind."

Rick only nodded as he replaced the lens cap as Becky nudged her horse ahead. He slowly slipped the camera back into the bag, buying himself some time, trying to find a place for the strange quiver of emotions she had aroused. Being attracted to a woman was nothing new. But he never felt this peculiar yearning mingling with the attraction. And he hadn't even kissed her yet.

Maybe that was the problem.

His horse shook its head, jangling the bridle, signaling its impatience with Rick's dithering. Rick untied the reins, toed his horse in the ribs and easily caught up to Becky.

He kept his distance, watching her from behind as if seeing her for the first time. Occasionally she would throw back a long look that pulled at him, but he stayed where he was. He wasn't sure what to do with the emotions she had raised in him with just one look. Just one touch.

He had nothing to compare this to. He had never been, what might be technically called, "in love" with any other woman before. In college his friends had often waxed poetic about other women and he'd dated a number of women there, but never more than a couple of times and never long enough to get to know them the way he knew Becky.

"You're mighty quiet back there," Becky said, angling her head back so he could hear her. "I hope I didn't make some major faux pas that I have to apologize for."

"Not yet."

Becky let her horse slow down until he came alongside her. "That's good, because I've been trying to figure out why you're not trying to start an argument with me."

"Some of us like to look around and enjoy the scenery maybe instead of talking all the time," he said, reaching for a teasing tone to his voice.

"Point taken. I'll be quiet."

"Think you can do it?"

"You're the one that's talking now."

And a reply would only underscore her rather childish comment, so he kept quiet. And as long as the trail was wide enough, she stayed beside him, distracting him with her silence this time, instead of her words.

Two hours later, they pulled their horses up in a shaded spot beside a brook that frothed and danced over a rock bed, a counterpoint to the murmuring and groaning of the other riders.

Rick slowly dismounted, his legs stiff from the ride. It had been over a year since he had ridden and he felt it in every muscle from his hips to his knees.

Some of the other riders looked relaxed, others hobbled around looking even worse than Rick felt.

"I didn't even know I had muscles in the places I'm feeling them," Becky moaned, slipping off her saddle. "I should have done some riding before this."

Rick moved around his horse to get her reins, but Trevor was right there. "Y'all okay, darlin'?" he drawled. "Saddle settin' okay?"

"You seem to have picked up a Texas accent to match your chaps," Becky said with a laugh. "And my saddle is fine."

"Jest playin' the part," he returned with a grin. "I'll tie up your horse. Go get something to drink or eat. Glenda will help you." Trevor glanced over Rick's horse. "How are you doin'? Everything good?"

"I'm okay." As if he'd admit to this cowboy that he was painfully aware of every muscle in his legs. "Beautiful ride."

"And more to come," Trevor promised, all business now, his accent slipping away. "If you want, you can ride up in front. I can give you a bit of history of the place, point out some scenic views you might miss on your own."

"I'm doing okay at the back," he said.

As Rick tightened up the cinch strap he glanced over the top of his horse at Becky.

Trevor intercepted the direction of his eyes. "She's quite a woman, isn't she? Always smiling, laughing. I don't think I've ever seen her angry."

Rick lashed his strap down, still watching Becky as he remembered hazel eyes snapping, that pert mouth tight with disapproval as they clashed over the direction of articles and the balance of advertising and content. "I have," he said with a wry grin.

Trevor took hold of Rick's saddle horn and tugged on it, as if testing it. "Becky is special to me, Rick." He held Rick's gaze, his own narrowed. "Just thought I'd mention that."

"That's interesting," Rick said, taking up the thinly veiled challenge as he dropped the stirrup, gentling his horse as it shied at the sudden movement. "She's never mentioned you."

Trevor laughed that off, patted Rick's horse on the neck and left. Rick watched him move directly to Becky as if to stake his claim, but Becky turned away as he came near.

Chapter Nine

The murmur of conversation faded away behind her as Becky picked her way through the trees, walking down a worn game trail. It was still light out and she wanted to grab a few moments of writing, away from people and chitchat and being perky and cheerful.

And watching out for Rick.

She lost track of how many times she'd glanced around looking for him, trying to keep her attention on the person talking to her, all the while searching out and finding Rick's blond hair. His easy smile.

A refreshing cool slipped down the valley, pockets of it captured in the wooded area close to the creek. The late-evening sun slanted through the trees, its light softened. The noise of the group behind her grew more muffled, with each step she took replaced by the quiet sigh of the forest.

She found a large rock still warm from the sun. She kicked off her boots and socks and sat down, pulling in a deep cleansing breath. The whisper of the leaves overhead were like a gentle prayer, the gurgle of the creek over the rocks a soft counterpoint. It was always outside that she felt most inspired, and this was a picture-perfect spot.

From the notebook she had packed, she pulled at the pages she had printed. She glanced over them, reading what she had done before.

As her eyes skimmed over what she had already written, the peace she felt just a scant moment ago fell away. Once her writing had seemed lively, fresh, but now the words dropped like stones, unwieldy and overdone.

Her pen slashed across the sentences, eradicating what offended her.

Which was about half. She read and reread what she had left and after a moment's thought scratched that out, too. Drivel. Dreck.

She set the printed pages aside and pulled out her notebook. Maybe she should just journal—maybe get some ideas for future "Runaround Sue" columns. She scribbled a few words, chasing an idea with her pen.

A thought gelled, took form.

Soon her pen was flowing across the page, her hand barely able to keep up with the ideas that burst through her mind. She had more than enough material for a couple of columns, but she couldn't stop the energy that flowed and crackled.

"Hey, there."

Becky's pen jerked across the page leaving a black streak. She spun around, her heart pushing against her throat in anticipation and confusion.

Rick stood behind her, hipshot, a camera slung around his neck, his hands strung up in the pockets of his blue jeans, a half smile teasing his lips.

"I'm sorry, I didn't mean to scare you." He strolled across the open space to where she sat, then leaned against her rock, glancing down at what she was writing. "Working already?"

Becky slapped the notebook shut, her racing heart a combination of her exciting writing spurt and Rick's presence.

"Just noodling," she said, willing her heart to slow. "Getting some ideas together. Just fooling around, really." And aren't you starting to sound like you have something to hide?

"You must be inspired. I tried to get your attention a couple of times."

Becky gave him a half shrug as if dismissing what she had been doing. "Sorry. I get a tunnel vision when I'm busy with something." Still holding the notebook, she pulled her knees up to her chin.

Rick said nothing in reply, but she was as aware of his presence beside her as if he were shouting.

"So how do the mountains of Alberta compare to other parts of the world?" she asked, anxious to remove the discomfort she felt in his presence. Idle chitchat became her fluttery defense.

"I'm often reminded of New Zealand."

Becky rested her chin on her knees, her eyes on the creek, but her attention straining toward the man beside her. "What places haven't you been that you'd like to see?"

"Let's see." Rick settled down on the stone beside her, his shoulder brushing against hers. "China is a mystery. I've only seen a few parts of it. The Antarctic. I haven't been to Peru yet or the Falklands. I'd love to go kayaking down to Baja and even though I've been there a couple of times, I'd love to go back to Italy."

"I liked the piece you did on hostels there." Becky sighed lightly. "Made me want to go there."

"Why don't you?"

"I don't think I'd like to travel alone, and most of my friends ended up moving away and getting married before they could commit to a trip. I suppose I could go if I really wanted to, but I'm usually too busy."

"Way too busy. I'm surprised you get as much done as you do."

"I have to write everything down." She blushed as she thought of her Day-Timer in his hands. "But you know that."

"How did you end up so involved?"

"We have a very active church, lots of young families. But they can't do a lot of the work because they are young families." She shrugged. "So someone needs to do the things that need to get done."

"And that someone seems to be you."

"I don't run the church single-handedly." Did she sound as if she did it all?

"No. But you seem to be carrying a lot of the burden."

"I just want to be a wise steward of the gifts God has given me."

Rick tapped the book on her lap. "And one of your gifts is this. Something you said yourself you don't spend enough time on."

You don't find time, you make time.

"I need to learn to trust in God to help me find the time."

"That may be," Rick said quietly. "But maybe you also need to learn to say no. To stop thinking if you don't do a job, it won't get done. If you do that, you might make more time for your writing. And maybe some traveling."

"Maybe I'm just a homebody."

Rick smiled at that. "Nothing wrong with that when you've got a good home to be in."

Becky turned her head toward him, wondering if she'd imagined the wistful tone in his voice.

"I've always been thankful for my home," she said quietly. "For the faith I was taught there, a faith that has grown over the years."

Rick's sigh drifted through the still air. "Well, that's another place you and I differ. Faith and family—neither have been a part of my life for a long time."

"But you grew up with it?"

Rick nodded. "I was taught all the right things, but traveling around the world, seeing the things I have..." He shrugged lightly. "Like I told your grandmother, I can't believe in a God that allows so much suffering."

Becky had heard this refrain so many times from people who wanted to ignore God, she was surprised Rick wasn't at least a little more original. "And what about what you're looking at now? What about this beautiful place? What about the people you've already met? What about all the good things that happen in the world?"

"What about it?"

"How can you not believe in a God who allows so much good? Who blesses us with so many good things? If you are going to acknowledge the one, you have to acknowledge the other."

Becky looked away, hoping, praying that God could

use her words. "Life is so incredibly complex and intertwined, so intricate. You just have to look at how an eye works, our lungs, our thoughts. Trees. Leaves. Photosynthesis." She stumbled over her words, trying to encapsulate Creation in the limited medium of conversation. "It's so amazing and breathtaking.... There's no way you can believe this just happened. And if it didn't just happen, then where did it come from? Who made it? And if you acknowledge that someone made it, you have to realize this was a great and powerful God who did—"

Becky felt Rick's hand on her shoulder. She stopped talking and turned to him.

"Such passion," he said softly. "You almost persuade me...."

Becky's breath caught in her throat. And she winged up another quick prayer. "I think you believe already, Rick. I think you just need to acknowledge that God cares about you. That He wants you to be a part of Him."

Rick tipped his head to one side. "And that's a problem, I'll admit."

Becky's heart brightened. It was small. But it was a start. *Please, Lord, help him let go. Help him to know that he needs Your saving grace.*

As their gazes met, a connection trembled between them, as real as a touch.

A faint breeze sifted down through the trees, catching Becky's hair and tossing it lightly across her cheeks. Rick reached out and tucked her hair behind her ear, letting his hand linger on her face.

This had to stop.

She put aside her notebook, jumped off the rock and headed out to the creek.

"What are you doing?" Rick called out.

Cooling off. Giving myself some breathing space.

"I just feel like wading." She carefully picked her way across the large stones, smoothed by centuries of water flowing over them.

"You're going to freeze your feet in that cold water. It's coming right off the glacier."

Becky ignored him and rolled up her jeans. She stepped out into the water and ice clutched her feet with numbing fingers. She sucked in her breath and took a few more halting steps, her arms flailing to catch her balance on feet she could hardly feel. This was ridiculous, but she wasn't going to back down.

"Look at me," Rick said. "I want to catch that expression on your face."

She spun around, holding her hand up in warning as she tottered on feet now totally devoid of feeling. "Don't you dare, Rick Ethier."

But he was already winding the camera. "I did dare." He walked closer and took another picture.

Becky bent over and scooped her hand through the water, spraying him.

Rick jerked his shoulder aside to protect his camera. When he turned back to her, his lopsided grin did not bode well.

He laid the camera down. "That was not a good idea, missy," he said, rolling up his sleeves. Too late she realized what he was going to do and tried to take a step away, but her ice-cold feet wouldn't respond. "I'm sorry, Rick."

"Too late for apologies."

He splashed toward her in his boots and before she could move again, he caught her around her shoulders, under her knees and swung her off her feet.

She shrieked and tried to fight him, but he was much stronger than she was.

"Put me down," she squealed, pushing against his chest as he waded farther out into the creek.

"That camera has been my constant companion for many years," he said, shaking his head. "Trying to make it wet was a declaration of war."

She grabbed on to his neck, fully conscious of the ice-cold water splashing below them. "If you drop me, I'll take you with."

He grinned down at her, his wide smile bracketed by dimples and lighting up his whole face. "That sounds like a challenge," he said softly.

"And you can never turn that down."

"How well you know me." Rick looked down at her but didn't move.

Becky had a sense of time wheeling around the two of them. Slowing. Rick's smile faded as their gazes locked, their breaths mingling. And then, without any forewarning, his lips touched hers, softly first, then more firmly.

Breathe, she reminded herself when he drew back, his eyes clouded now with an indefinable emotion. His eyes flicked over her face, as if seeking some clue there as to what had just happened.

In silence he touched his lips to hers again, then turned and strode back with her to the rock she had been sitting on. He set her down as carefully as if she were some fragile creature. Then he knelt down beside her, brushing her hair unnecessarily back from her face, his fingers trailing down the side of her face.

Becky caught his hand. As she pressed it to her cheek, confusion wrestled with attraction.

This was wonderful.

This wasn't a good idea.

He wasn't on the same level spiritually as she was.

He was seeking.

She lowered his hand to her lap, and held it there. On the back of his hand was a faint star-shaped scar. She traced it lightly again and again as she tried to put these new emotions into the proper place in her life. Her mind told her one thing, her heart another.

A heart that had never been touched like this. It scared her that it was Rick, temporary and negative, who had been the one to do so.

"Is something wrong, Becky?" he asked, tipping her chin up with his other hand. "You're so quiet."

"I'm not sure what to do. How to feel." She laughed lightly, suddenly self-conscious as she looked up at him. "I'm not the casual dating type, Rick. I never wanted to fall into that pattern."

"I know." Rick stroked her chin with his thumb, a serious cast to his expression. "Your grandmother sent me a not so veiled warning where you were concerned."

"She would." Becky tried to laugh, to ease the tension that gripped her heart.

"So this is where I should apologize for kissing you."

"Why?"

Rick hunkered back on his heels and picked up her foot. "Because if you don't believe in casual dating, you don't believe in casual kissing." He started massaging her foot, which only succeeded in heightening Becky's confusion.

"Was that what that was? A casual kiss?"

Rick kept his head bent over her feet. "I don't know what it was, Becky." He rubbed her foot harder. "My goodness, girl. Your feet are like ice."

Becky let it go. She was too confused to even know which emotion to track down. Which feeling was real. With Rick she had to depend on her head to guide her. Not her heart.

"You did warn me about the cold water," she said, moving the conversation to a safer place.

"Some people have to find things out the hard way, I guess."

He took her other foot in his hands and rubbed it, too, bringing the circulation back.

"What about you? You got your boots wet. The bottom of your pants, too."

Rick shrugged her concerns away. "These boots have been in water before. I'll dry them at the campfire." Rick lowered her foot and picked up her shoes and socks. "At least yours are dry."

"At least if I'm going wading, I do some planning." She slipped her socks on, thankful for the return to the usual conversational mode.

"Spontaneity is the spice of life." Rick stood and helped her off the rock. "Don't forget your notebook."

"And you don't forget your camera."

Rick shook his head. "Have to have the last word, don't you?"

But Becky just smiled back in spite of everything and

picked up her notebook. Once again Rick had put her in a self-defeating position.

The night sky was endless.

If he looked at the scattered stars long enough, he could get lost, sucked into the vast depths of a universe unmeasured and incomprehensible by man's tiny mind.

Better to stay grounded here, lying on the plain, hard dirt. Rick sighed lightly, tucking his hands behind his head, tracing the constellations in the sky as the point of a rock dug into his hip.

God's creation.

He could still hear Becky's exuberant voice challenging him not to believe in God when His hand was so evident.

It wasn't that Rick didn't believe in God. He just wished he could understand Him a little better. Could feel like he, Rick, deserved to be a part of God's community.

A sliver of light streaked silently across the sky and Rick smiled, wishing Becky could have seen it. She would have expressed the appropriate awe instead of figuring out the purpose of pieces of rock burning up through the atmosphere.

Maybe he needed to stop critiquing and listen more. Maybe he needed to go looking for God, instead of waiting for his questions to be answered.

Rick yawned and pushed himself off the ground, glancing once more at the vast sky above him. Fragments of a Bible verse came back to him.

"When I consider the heavens...the works of Your hands...what is man that Thou art mindful of Him..."

What indeed?

* * *

Rick swung the saddle on his horse, his gaze sweeping the campsite as he did. How easily he found her. Like his internal radar had an automatic "Becky" setting.

She was washing up the dishes from breakfast in the central opening of camp, chatting and laughing with the two women helping her. She wore her hair up this morning, emphasizing the delicate bone structure of her face. At that moment she looked up and found him. A tentative smile edged her lips but then she glanced away again.

All morning she had kept her distance from him and he had respected it, but all morning he found himself hearing only her voice above other voices. Seeing only her face.

His horse nudged his shoulder with his head, as if pulling his attention to the job at hand. Rick laughed to himself and bent down to bring the cinch up and around. With a few flips of the latigo he had it on enough to hold it for now. He would tighten it before they left.

Becky was gone.

Which was just as well. He did have work to do.

He loaded up his camera and walked around. He already had seven rolls' worth of pictures, but he wanted to make sure he had captured the obvious enthusiasm the people had for this trip.

It was his last opportunity. When the group headed out farther up the valley, he and Becky and their guide would return to the ranch.

He wanted to stay here, in this place away from the office, away from the stress and pressures of the magazine and its relentless deadlines.

He wanted to go back to the creek and sit with Becky

and talk to her. Try to capture her optimistic faith, her enthusiasm for life. She was the first woman he had met who wasn't afraid to stand up to him and who could make him laugh—sometimes both at the same time.

She was the first woman who could steal his breath with one look.

Rick tried to reason his way past his growing attraction to her. But nothing fit his usual reasons. Yes, she was pretty. Yes, she was fun. Yes, she could laugh.

She had depth, a grounding in her personal life and in her religious life. She wasn't afraid to talk about her faith. Nor to challenge him to take a second look at his own lack. She had an utter confidence in who she was.

It drew him on even as it frightened him away.

He walked around the string of packhorses, seeing it through the lens of his camera as the wranglers weighed the boxes, balanced the loads and hung them on the animals.

A few flies buzzed around in the cool morning air. The horses blew and stomped their hooves, as if anxious to be off, while the men threw tarps over their packs. Then they lashed them down, wrapping the ropes in an intricate pattern, working in a harmony that looked like a dance.

"You want to learn how to throw a diamond?"

Rick lowered his camera and glanced sidelong at Trevor who stood beside him, holding a length of soft rope.

It was on the tip of his tongue to refuse. He didn't need to prove himself. Then he caught the faint challenge in Trevor's eyes.

"That would be interesting." Rick covered his camera up and took it off his neck, looking for a place to set it.

"I'll take it." Becky was beside him, her hand held out. "If you can trust me with it." Her smile was like a light, drawing him on.

Suddenly the day was brighter.

"I don't know." He smiled back, picking up her infectious humor. "You tried to drown it yesterday."

Becky pressed one hand on her heart. "I promise I will treat it with the respect your constant companion deserves."

"You're sounding a little disrespectful right now," he said, letting go of the camera.

"And you are a suspicious man." Mischief glinted in her eyes, and he had to laugh.

"And you always have to have the last word."

"This is really cute, but the horses are waiting," Trevor broke in, sounding impatient.

"Lead the way," Rick said, not responding to Becky's saucy wink.

In spite of his pique, Trevor was a patient teacher. Rick gained a new appreciation of the science of packing horses as he learned to balance the weight of the load and lay down the ropes over the tarp.

"You want the tension of the rope spread evenly over the whole pack," Trevor explained as he stood beside Rick, showing him how to tighten the ropes. "The horse feels more comfortable and that makes him less likely to go ballistic in the middle of a bog. A well tied pack saves you from fishin' instant-porridge packages out the water."

"Sounds like a good incentive."

"So all you need to do is tighten 'er up." Trevor made a motion to the wrangler on the other side of the pack-horse and Rick followed his rhythm as they took turns pulling on the rope.

Trevor showed Rick how to tie the knot and the job was done.

"Hey, boys, how about a smile?" Becky called out.

Rick looked up just in time to see Becky's face obscured by the camera.

"Don't waste film, Becky," he called out, holding up his hand.

"Too late. This is the fourth picture." Becky lowered the camera, grinning at the two of them. "And now the film is full."

She handed him the camera with a wink, spun on her heel and walked away. And Rick's gaze followed her every step.

Half an hour later, the group mounted up and Rick shot some final pictures as the group left them, waving and laughing. Before he became publisher of a magazine, he could have simply mounted up and followed them, making decisions on the fly. But now he had obligations waiting.

Hopefully only a few more months and that would be over, as well. But as he turned around, he saw Becky sitting on her horse, waiting for him to accompany her and the wrangler who was to guide them back. Back to responsibilities and decisions that dragged him down and pinned him here.

He felt as if he stood at a pivotal point—his past moving away from him deeper into the mountains—his future represented by Becky and the magazine.

It frightened him. For the first time in his life he didn't know which called him stronger.

He swung onto his horse and without waiting for Becky, he urged it on down the path. Back to the ranch and back to Okotoks.

But as he rode, Becky's presence hovered behind him, an allure that battled with his desire for freedom. He stayed ahead of her, as if trying to outrun it.

Chapter Ten

"Rick back yet?" Becky leaned on the divider, hoping her voice sounded more nonchalant than she felt.

Trixie glanced up from her computer and slowly shook her head. "Sorry, babe. All I got was a call on Tuesday night at home saying he was going to be gone a few days." Trixie's eyes were full of sympathy and Becky knew, with a sinking heart, that her attraction to Rick was growing more obvious.

"Okay. I suppose he'll call if he has anything to tell me." Becky gave Trixie a tight smile, scooped up her mail and walked down the hall. Her steps slowed as she passed Rick's office. The door was closed as it had been for the past two days.

They had made good time coming back down the valley. Rick had been in the lead and set a brisk pace. Once in a while he would stop to take pictures, but even then he didn't speak to her. Becky gave up trying to catch up. When they got back to the ranch he had his horse unsaddled and the tack taken care of before she had barely dismounted. He was gone while she was still walking her horse. The next day she had come to the office early, hoping to talk to him.

All that was waiting for her was a cryptic note in Rick's bold handwriting lying on her desk.

"Gone for a few days. Be back day after tomorrow."

As she dropped into her seat she looked out the window, her gaze drawn to the ridge of mountains on the horizon, as if she could find the answer to Rick's elusive behavior there. Resting her chin on her hands, she let her mind wander back to those few magical days they had spent together. Correction, one day. What had happened the second day still bewildered her. It had started out so promising. Then, when it was time for them to go back, the very act of turning around had shifted his attention away from her.

She could still see him, leaning forward in the saddle, as if moving toward something. Or away from her?

Her fingers brushed her lips, reliving his kiss. A kiss that had buried itself deep in her heart. The kiss that had sent her heart soaring, her mind following.

He's going.

Reality knifed through the soft daydreams she had spun. How could she be so foolish?

Her eyes drifted closed, her heart reaching out to the one secure love in her life.

Oh, Lord, am I attaching too much importance to one simple gesture? Should I have stopped him?

But even as she prayed, she felt his hand on her cheek, saw his head bent over her feet, felt his hands rubbing warmth back into them.

She pressed her hand to her heart as if to hold it steady. Keep it captive. Because to give it to Rick was to open herself to pain and heartbreak. Yet how could she ignore the surge of her heart whenever she saw him? The tangible connection she felt whenever they spoke?

She had never felt this way around a man. Was she so shallow as to fall for someone whose smile lit up his whole face? Whose eyes delved deep into her soul?

She yanked open the drawer beside her and pulled out her Bible, seeking comfort from the familiar words. As her fingers flipped through the pages she stopped at Psalm 52, drawing the words into her heart, allowing them to take root.

"But I am like a healthy olive tree. My roots are deep in the house of God. I trust in Your faithful love forever and ever."

The words reminded her that she was first and foremost a child of God. That she was grounded in His unfailing love and salvation. He was always faithful, always there, always loving.

Forgive me, Lord, she prayed. She closed her eyes and drew in a long slow breath.

Then jumped when she felt a hand drop on her shoulder. She jerked her head up and started inwardly when she looked into Rick's face. A ghost of a smile drifted over his lips, and his eyes softened as he looked down on her.

Relax. Breathe.

"Hey, there," he said, his voice washing over her like rain on parched ground. "How are you?"

Remember what you just read. You are a child of God. Rooted and grounded in Him.

"I'm doing fine."

As if sensing the detachment in her voice, he removed his hand. "Did you get my note? Sorry I didn't phone."

"I'm not your boss. Or your keeper." The words were harsh, but it was too late to retract or rephrase.

Let it lie. Better if you create some distance.

Rick took a step back, surprise creeping over his face. He moved around to the front of her desk and stood there as if waiting for something more.

Becky pressed her lips together, holding back the questions begging to be let out. Where were you? Why did you run away? Why didn't you call?

One kiss, a few glances exchanged did not give her any rights.

"Have you had a chance to work on the article for the trail ride?" he asked, slipping his hands into the pockets of his blue jeans in a gesture of retreat.

"I've been run off my feet, but I did have a chance to rough it out. I can print out what I have if you want to have a look at it."

So casual. So cold and unfeeling. It was as if that moment at the creek had never even happened. It was what she wanted, wasn't it?

He nodded, a quick jerk of his head. "There's no rush. Whenever you're ready. I've got the pictures on it already." He paused a moment, as if he wanted to say something, but then turned and left.

The click of the door resounded through the quiet of Becky's office and in spite of her self-talk, all her good intentions, the harshness of that sound cut her to the core.

And for once she was thankful for the relentless deadlines of her work that kept her tired mind busy and distracted from the confusion Rick posed.

She stifled a tired yawn and went back to work.

* * *

He should have called her. Rick knew that now. But when he jumped into his Jeep that evening, the only thing on his mind was running. Leaving. Finding some breathing room. He didn't *have* to meet with that marketing advisor in Calgary. Nor did he *have* to head up to Edmonton to get some quotes from a printing company.

Becky had given him much to think about and he needed time to sort it out. Find a place for it in his life. Figure out what to do with it.

He dropped into his chair, spun it around so it faced the window. He then lifted his feet to rest on the low sill. All he could see from this position were the mountains where he had just spent two days that had spun his world around, rearranged all his plans and expectations.

One kiss. That was all they had shared but that was all it took to make him realize that Becky had become integral to his life.

And that was what made him run. She represented security. Stability. Numbing routine.

God.

Rick closed his eyes a moment, remembering her passion when she talked about Creation. And once again what she said spoke to a deeper part of him. He knew God existed. He knew God was there.

It was easy to believe in God around Becky. Harder when he was on his own. All the accusations he had hurled at God when he was alone in his bedroom, wishing that he still had his mother, came hurtling back. Surely God didn't want to have anything to do with someone who was angry with Him?

How can you not believe in a God who allows so much good?

Rick hadn't been able to erase those words from his mind. They spun, whirled and at the same time comforted. Against his will, Becky was showing him a different side of God. A side he never saw in his grandfather.

So what do I do now, Lord? I'm allowed to ask You the hard questions. So why do You allow suffering? Why do You let people be lonely and hurt?

He waited, listening.

Nothing. Not surprising.

With a heavy sigh, he half turned, grabbing the envelope of pictures off the desk. He had just gotten them developed. A lot of magazines used digital cameras, but he preferred the clarity of analog.

He opened the envelope, pulled out the pictures and started flipping through them. Ranch house. Outbuildings. More buildings. Trevor in full cowboy mode.

Becky.

He stopped, lifting the picture to get a better look.

She was looking at him, a light frown crinkling her forehead. In the next picture she was smiling.

He set them aside and flipped quickly through the rest. The lighting had been perfect, showing the mountains in all their glory. Some of the pictures could almost be called cliché mountain shots, but he had managed to zoom in and isolate some of the views, creating a different look.

They would look great in the magazine.

There's no way you can believe this just happened. As Becky's challenge to him strayed into his mind, he turned to the next picture. And his heart quickened.

Becky astride a horse, framed against an achingly blue sky, the mountains a mere backdrop to her beauty. The wind had lifted her hair from her face so that it framed her delicate features in an aureole of auburn. She was smiling—a full-featured Becky smile that came from deep within her.

Rick leaned back, touching Becky's face with one finger as if trying to resurrect her, resurrect the emotions that had arced between them that moment at the creek, at her father's orchard.

He should have told her where he'd been the past few days, but that would mean telling her why he had run off. Which would mean delving into reasons that frightened and exhilarated him at the same time.

Reasons that involved Becky and feelings that had changed from simple acknowledgment of her good looks, to admiration for her spunk and ability to stand up to him, to respect for her deep faith to something deeper and unidentifiable.

Something that trembled at the edge of his consciousness, luring him into a place he had never been before.

A place that was a curious combination of love and faith.

He flipped through the rest of the pictures, sorting them out into their various groupings. Scenery. People. Horses.

Becky.

Becky doing dishes. Becky laughing and chatting with a group of people. Becky wading in the creek, her teeth clenched against the cold.

Becky warning him not to take the picture he was now looking at.

He turned around and propped the picture against his telephone, remembering what had followed that moment. How she had touched his heart in so many ways.

So what next?

He knew he messed up when he took off without telling her, and now she was ticked off.

Might be better that way. They would slowly move away from each other, keeping their relationship purely professional, and when it was time for him to leave there would be no hard feelings.

So why did the thought leave an empty ache in his heart?

The light knock at the door was a welcome intrusion to thoughts that spun, unresolved. Trixie put her head around the corner. "Mr. McElroy to see you about the advertorial you were going to put in an upcoming issue?"

And Rick was dropped back into the turning around of a magazine. His ticket out of this town.

"I thought the focus of the article was the business aspect." Rick tapped his pen against his chin as he skimmed over the pages Becky had given him. She had dropped the article on his desk late last night, with a brief note asking for his input.

So now he was giving it and she didn't look pleased.

"I thought I brought in enough of the business angle, by maintaining the history of the ranch and how it got to the current owners and their involvement in the community."

"I think they were looking for a heavier slant."

Becky's sigh clearly telegraphed to him that she was

going to dig in her heels. And to his own surprise, he was looking forward to what she had to say. Anytime they'd struggled over articles, they'd found a compromise which, surprisingly, made for a stronger article than either of them would have written alone.

"We were invited by Triple Bar J to go riding in the mountains, Rick, surrounded by God's wonderful and amazing creation. Unless they're paying to do the entire article, I think we better stick with more of a story slant to the article."

Becky slouched back in her chair, her arms folded over her chest, staring blankly at the window behind him with her head against the back of the chair. She looked totally disinterested.

He didn't have to be literate to read her body language.

With a sinking heart he realized they were back to where they had started the very first day he had met her here in Nelson's office. For a moment he was tempted to pull out the picture of her that he had gotten enlarged, just to remind himself that there was another time and another place when she had smiled at him. When she had kissed him.

He blinked the thoughts away, dragging his attention back to the article. "It's not an advertorial, but they did invite us free of charge. Besides, every event can be slanted in a certain way to highlight the things you want to say. In this case you might want to focus on who is involved in the trail ride and what brings them there. Who they are and what businesses they represent."

He didn't look up, preferring to look at her words rather than her face. Easier to read what he wanted into

the black-and-white medium of paper and ink. She
didn't say anything so he continued.

"Your descriptions are evocative. You have a way
with words." What she had given him had a wonderful
flow that he didn't want to break up, yet he knew he had
to emphasize the business aspect of the company. That
was his focus for *Going West*.

He tapped the paper with his pen, thinking, trying to
find a compromise that would work for either of them,
surprised she hadn't challenged him again.

"I suppose we could work the business aspect into a
sidebar. Expand on it there without losing the integrity
of what you've written. What do you think?"

He waited for her comment on this concession and
when none came, he looked up.

She was asleep.

Rick rested his elbows on his desk and leaned forward, watching her. Allowing himself this moment to
let his eyes pass over her face, to remember her smile.

Her head drifted to one side, then jerked.

Staying in the chair would give her a horrible crick
in her neck, but he didn't want to wake her up.

He got up and cleared off the couch, then walked
back to her side. Carefully, so as not to wake her, he fitted his arm under her knees, around her shoulders and
carefully picked her up. It was only a few steps to the
couch, but he moved slowly, afraid to wake her. Afraid
to let go of her.

She shifted in his arms, and he gently laid her down.
She stretched out, groaned, then muttered a few words,
frowning in her sleep as she flopped over onto her side.

Her hair had fallen across her face and her lips

twitched as if in annoyance. Rick took a chance and carefully brushed her hair back, once again allowing his hand to linger on the soft curve of her cheek.

He knew he was treading on dangerous ground, but he couldn't stop himself. She shifted on the couch, pulling her arm up beside her face then, incredibly, a smile tugged at her lips.

He felt a clench of longing and, giving in to an impulse, bent over and brushed his lips over her forehead, inhaling the soft sweet scent of her hair, her skin.

He sat back on his heels, laughing shortly at his own foolish impulse, then got up and walked back to his desk. He grabbed her article and took it out of the office. He could just as easily look it over in the coffee shop across the way.

But before he closed the door, he chanced one more look at Becky.

Her eyes were open and she was watching him.

"So far, our subscriptions are slowly moving up. I guess the ad campaign is doing what it was supposed to, but we're still bleeding red ink." Trixie handed Rick and Becky each some papers stapled together. "You'll see that we've spent a lot more on drumming up new business in the last quarter."

Becky chewed on her bottom lip as she looked over the figures. Numbers weren't her strong point, but it didn't take a degree in accounting to compare figures and know that they were falling behind.

"Our own advertising income is slowly increasing and I know we've picked up a few more accounts," Rick put in from his perch on the edge of his desk, swinging his foot back and forth. He seldom sat down during their business meetings. He was often pacing around, talking aloud, urging the sales force on, challenging the art department and placating Trixie. "Subscriptions are edging up. I think we're getting close. If we can up the advertising, we can get a better influx of cash."

"But we still have to maintain a balance between ads and content," Becky said, glancing over the rest of the figures. "People buy the magazine because of the teasers on the cover. And if they have to go burrowing through twenty pages of ads in order to get to what they were looking for you're going to get frustrated readers. Which doesn't translate into increased subscriptions."

"But we need the ads for revenue. And they need space."

Becky looked up at him, her momentary pique tempered by a gentle thrill when she caught his eye. So easily she felt again the touch of his lips on her forehead.

He held her gaze, those same lips softening in a gentle smile.

Focus, Becky, focus. Your job is on the line here. This magazine can't keep operating in the red.

"People are willing to put up with a certain amount of advertising to read articles with good content. Cut that back and you're going to see your subscriptions go down. When that happens, ad revenues go down."

Rick's lazy smile kicked her heart up a notch, but she held his gaze, determined to keep this part of her life professional.

"A tricky balancing act," Rick said softly.

She wondered if his comment was as innocent as a mere agreement. No matter. She was still an editor. He was still a publisher. And though the lines were growing increasingly blurred, she was determined to keep her focus when she could.

"It can be done," she said, lifting her chin a notch. "If there's a vision to see growth over the long term, rather than short. And if we are willing to slow the pace of the change."

"Commitment, in other words."

Becky frowned, sensing a wealth of meaning beneath the simple comment. But she wasn't going to go fishing in that pool. She looked back down at the paper. "I want to keep this job for a long time, so obviously my focus, my vision for *Going West,* is slow but steady growth."

Rick blew out his breath in a long sigh but Becky kept her eyes down.

"How ever we look at it, we're going to need a better month than this one. For the next month we've got a good lineup but I'm pretty sure the month after that is going to be the turning point." Rick paused, as if waiting to get Becky's attention. She reluctantly looked back at him.

"Do you have the interview with the premier sewn up?"

"All set for this Thursday." She held his gaze and once again felt an involuntary quiver.

"Good. That, combined with the Triple J ride, will give the magazine some meat. Excellent."

He didn't exactly rub his hands, but Becky easily sensed his enthusiasm and excitement. How could he be so positive when things looked so bleak for the magazine? *Going West* had seen tough times during Nelson's tenure, but never had they been so far down financially as they were now.

"In the meantime, we still have a serious cash-flow problem, Rick," Trixie said. "We need to figure out how to solve that."

Becky's earlier thrill was washed away by a rush of dread. This magazine might be just a project to Rick, but for her it was her livelihood until she sold her book. But to sell, she had to finish—and how was she going to find time to do that?

"Well, I'll see what we can do about that." Rick jumped off the desk, seemingly unfazed by this new disaster. And why should he be? If the magazine failed he would move back to Toronto and work for his grandfather.

She would be stuck back here in Okotoks trying to figure out how to make a living.

And trying to figure out if she could live without Rick.

"I'm on my way to an important interview right now, Terry. I can't come to the bank." Rick spun the steering wheel one-handed around the corner and glanced at Becky who was trying not to look as if she was listening to the conversation. "Well, let me know as soon as you find out. And don't forget, Terry, this magazine is going to go places. Don't bail on me."

He disconnected and dropped his phone into a pocket of his vest, stifling his impatience.

"I'm guessing that was the bank," Becky said after a moment.

Rick shook his head in disgust. "Terry is getting antsy. He wanted me to come to a meeting to justify the bank's extending our line of credit. A few years ago banks gave away loans like they were popcorn prizes.

Now, even though they are still making record profits, they're going into deep miser mode."

Thankfully Becky said nothing. He didn't want to talk about the magazine's financial woes. Not when he was on his way to an interview that had the potential to change everything.

He came to a halt at a quiet intersection. "Where do we go from here?"

"Follow the road along the ravine until you come to a cul-de-sac. He lives at the end."

The homes grew farther apart as they drove. Not the wealthiest section of the city, but money was definitely in evidence here. Old and new money from the looks of the houses and the towering elm trees sheltering the road.

The whole effect was one of seclusion and genteel country right in the middle of the city.

They parked in front of the house and were greeted by a tall, unsmiling man who checked them over.

"Where's your notepad?" Rick whispered as they were led to the back of the premier's house.

"I'm not going to write things down. I'm just going to use the tape."

"Backup, Becky. You know the first rule of journalism." Rick caught her arm just before they entered the backyard. "You're not going to catch everything." Was she trying to sabotage this interview?

"Maybe not, but I think he'll be more relaxed if I'm not scribbling down everything he says. Makes it look like I'm not listening if I do that." Becky flashed a smile at Rick but at the same time she tried to pull her arm free.

Rick wasn't ready to let go of her yet. "Do you mind if I write something down?"

"You'll be too busy taking pictures." Becky stopped pulling, but looked away from him. "Please trust me to do this interview my way, Rick," she said softly.

Rick reluctantly let go of her arm and reluctantly agreed.

Jake, dressed casually in jeans and a golf shirt, sat at a patio table. He looked tanned, fit and in charge. But when he saw Becky, his smile lit up his face, giving him the boyish charm that made many a single woman's heart beat just a little faster.

That the same charm was directed at Becky gave Rick the same foolish twinge of jealousy he felt around Trevor.

Becky introduced Rick and he noticed Jake's polite but forced smile. Noticed a sudden wariness. "I've read a number of your articles, Rick," he said, the polite heartiness in his voice the hallmark of a good politician. "Very insightful, though at times negative."

"Not what you're going to see in *Going West,*" Becky said, glancing nervously from one to the other. "We're interested in getting to know you as a person." Becky laughed lightly, touching Jake on the arm, drawing his attention back to her. "Because I know another side of you that you don't always let out."

Jake flashed his smile back at Becky now. "Glad to hear that. Shall we sit down?" Jake waved to the table he had been sitting at.

"You know what, Jake? It's such a lovely yard. Why don't you show me around it?" Becky said with a quick smile, looking around the immaculately groomed yard. "I recognize some of the same plants Dad has, but others are different."

Though the yard didn't have the same vigor and charm that Becky's father's had, it was still a showpiece. Flowers and shrubs edged a large expanse of golf-course grass. A cedar gazebo was tucked away in a far corner against tall trees, also edged with flower gardens.

"You don't have the fountain yet," Becky commented as they strolled down an inlaid brick path that broke up the lawn.

"That's coming soon. I'm not sure what kind to put in."

"You take care of this yard yourself?" Rick asked, slipping the covers off the lenses of his cameras. He had two slung around his neck, each with different lenses giving him a variety of options.

"When I have time. I employ a gardener during spring session of the legislature, but when I'm not traveling I try to spend time here."

"Is that an Intrigue rose?" Becky stopped by a rounded bush resplendent with deep purple-red, showy roses, and dropped to one knee. She bent over, touching a flower with one hand, inhaling deeply. "Oh, smell that. Very strong citrus smell. Where did you get this one? My dad's been itching to get one for a while now."

"Hole's Greenhouse in Edmonton. I got the last one a year ago."

"Amazing." Becky smiled and gently touched one of the flowers. "They are so beautiful."

Jake hunkered down beside her, and as they chatted about the pros and cons of raising tender roses in a prairie climate, Rick went to work snapping pictures. He worked carefully, trying to remain inconspicuous as possible, yet listening at the same time.

They moved on to some of his other flowering plants.

Rick was lost in all the talk about pruning, mulching, bone meal and dividing, but Becky had complete control of the conversation at all times. She gently led Jake from a discussion on sedum to environmental issues, from admiring his lilies to health-care funding. Rick couldn't help but admire her style.

She pitched her voice a few notes lower, creating an air of intimacy. She made eye contact frequently, occasionally touching Jake on the arm to underline a question or a point. Each time he spoke she leaned forward ever so slightly, showing him that he had her complete attention.

And the most interesting part of it all, Rick knew that with Becky it wasn't just a game. A way of getting information from this elusive man. It was a genuine interest in his hobby, in him as a person.

By the time they had gone through the garden, and were sitting at the patio table with a glass of lemonade in front of each of them, Jake looked far more relaxed than he had when they began the interview. Rick positioned them for a photo so they were facing each other with Jake's chair slightly angled away from where Rick had planned on sitting. He wanted to be able to listen but at the same time be as unobtrusive as possible.

"I think it's fascinating how you're trying to focus on native prairie plants. I should get my father to partner with you on that," Becky said as she casually dropped her tape recorder on the table. "I'll need to record this. Do you mind?" she asked, gesturing to it as she flicked it on.

Jake waved her question aside with a casual flick of his hand. "I had envisioned working with private business on that rather than creating yet another government bureaucracy. I think if we can get enough people to catch the vision, we can expand the program and make it self-funding."

Jake was leaning forward now, his attention fully engaged on Becky, which is just what Rick wanted. Becky had forged an uncanny connection with the premier and in spite of his own faint jealousy, he knew that connection was going to make the difference between a bland interview and one that sparkled and surprised.

So he took a few pictures, then returned to his seat, content to be ignored, but listening intently to everything that was said, jotting down relevant notes.

The interview ranged from his plans to reduce government red-tape to encouraging new Alberta-based value-added business to more social issues. As they spoke, Rick felt a growing impatience with Becky's style. Sure the premier was opening up to her, but as he had clearly stated initially, the interview was starting to ramble.

He tried to catch Becky's eye, to warn her, but she steadfastly ignored him, her entire attention on Jake.

They were now talking about family values. An older, outdated subject, but Becky seemed to warm to it.

"I think it's important that we support the traditional family unit," Jake was saying, "but at the same time we need to recognize that there are many single-parent families who are coping with a tremendous amount of pressure."

This was *not Going West's* focus at all. Rick raised his camera and took a few pictures, then glanced over it when he saw he had caught Becky's attention. He shook his head slightly and pivoted his finger in a circle, a subtle reminder to get back to the point.

Becky turned back to the premier, ignoring Rick. She asked a few more questions pertaining to family, made a few comments, and as they chatted, Rick could sense she was winding the interview down.

He shifted in his seat, impatient with Becky. They had talked about what they were going to do with this. What their focus was going to be. She had barely touched on the topics he needed covered. How was she going to glean anything of substance, anything different from a thousand other interviews that would set this one apart?

Sure, they had been invited into his yard. Sure, he had some pet project that they could maybe focus on, but what was that?

Then he caught a different note in Jake's tone. A subtle shift in his body language.

Jake was getting comfortable. And personal.

Now they were getting somewhere.

"People need to take responsibility for their actions, Becky," he was saying. Rick felt the hairs on his neck go up and he straightened, straining to hear what Jake was saying.

"I know I've been remiss in that department."

Becky leaned closer, touching him on the arm again. She was no longer the interviewer. She had become a friend. Confidante.

How had she done that?

He didn't care. He had become hyperaware of the change in the atmosphere and was watching Jake like a hawk.

"What are you trying to say, Jake?"

He sighed and dragged a hand over his face. "I know I shouldn't be saying this on the news. You're a reporter."

"I'm also your friend."

Jake laughed lightly. "That's a rarity for someone like me. I guess what I've always appreciated about you, Becky, was the fact that you were never fazed by the idea that I am premier. That I hold power."

"Your power is given you by God. You're holding it, yes, but in trust. I serve the same God but in a different capacity. We're equal that way." Becky smiled gently at him. "And as for the fact that you're single—" she winked at him, then glanced at Rick "—that has never been a factor."

Rick held her gaze a moment, wondering what she was saying.

"I've often seen you alone at functions. No boyfriend?"

Again Becky's glance slid to Rick's then away as if she wasn't sure where to put him in her life.

He had kissed her. Had flirted with her.

She shook her head. "How about you? Any significant others in your life?" she asked, her attention focused back on Jake. "You're seen with a different woman just about every time you step out."

Jake waggled his hand. "You know how it is, Becky. I have functions I have to attend. I can't come alone so I find someone. Or get my assistant to find someone. Usually a friend of a friend. Often a married woman to help me avoid any personal entanglements."

"I remember a girl named Kerra. You've mentioned her once or twice."

Kerra? Becky knew about a "personal entanglement" named Kerra? How had she known and why hadn't she told him this?

Jake shifted in his chair, his hand stroking his chin

as he seemed to be looking past Becky into the middle distance. His body language was so different from when they had first come that Rick could only be amazed at the transformation of the high-comfort level Jake felt with Becky.

The vibration in his pocket made him jump. He glanced at Becky and Jake, but they weren't even paying attention to him. It was as if they had forgotten he was there.

Rick slowly drew the phone out of his pocket. It was Terry, their accounts manager.

Chapter Eleven

Rick glanced at the tape recorder on the table between Jake and Becky. Still running. He didn't want to take this call, but he had to. He carefully got up from the table and walked to the back of the yard, out of earshot of Becky and Jake.

"I hope you've got good news, Terry?"

"I tried, Rick, but there's no way they're going to extend credit unless the magazine comes up with some kind of security."

"Terry, if we had security, we wouldn't need an extension," Rick felt like yelling.

"One of the managers suggested you talk to your grandfather. Surely with his substantial assets..."

"Forget it. There's no way I'm going to Colson Ethier to beg for spare change." The very thought. "You know the only reason I let things get this far is because when I first came to you, you virtually assured me that I would be able to access this money. *'No problem'* were your words. If I had known you were going to get spineless on me, I wouldn't have put out the money I did." Rick shoved his hand through his hair in frustration. "So who do I need to talk to?"

"I did what I could, Rick."

"No, you didn't, Terry. Give me a name and a number." Rick flipped a page over on the pad of paper he had in his pocket and scribbled the name Terry gave him.

"I don't know if it's going to make a difference," Terry protested.

"I'm Colson Ethier's grandson, Terry. Trust me. It will make a difference." It galled Rick to drop his grandfather's name, but he was getting desperate. Better to use Colson's name than his money. This magazine had to make it on its own. "Arrange it. I'll hold."

Rick glanced over at Becky, who was still leaning close to the premier, their heads bent. What were they doing? Praying?

He wanted to be there, but from what he could see, Becky hadn't turned the tape off. He could listen to it later. He had to deal with this while he still had some breathing room.

A few minutes later Terry had the meeting arranged.

As Rick rang off, he strode to the table. Becky looked up as he came and she got to her feet.

"Time to go?" Becky asked.

Rick frowned. "Not unless you're done here?"

Becky nodded and turned the tape recorder off. She dropped it casually in her purse. She gave Rick only a brief glance before turning back to Jake. "Thanks so much for taking the time to see us." She touched him again. "You take care. I'll be praying for you."

Jake laughed lightly. "And coming from you, I know

that's not just casual talk. Thanks, Becky." He bent over and kissed her lightly on the forehead.

And Rick's jealousy battled with curiosity. What had they talked about while he was trying to save the magazine? He'd just have to wait until he could hear what was on the tape recorder.

Jake glanced at his watch. "I have another appointment, so I have to run. It was good to see you again, Becky." Jake turned to Rick and held out his hand. "It was a pleasure to meet you, too, Rick."

"Thanks for your time, Mr. Premier," Rick said, shaking Jake's hand. "We're most appreciative."

"I'd like to see a copy of the interview before you put it into print," Jake said, slipping his hands into his pockets. "Dilton is going to be having ulcers until he sees it. He didn't want me to do the interview in the first place."

"I doubt it..."

"Of course..."

Rick and Becky spoke at the same time. Rick shot Becky a warning look, which she returned with puzzlement.

"What I can do is discuss the angle we'll be taking before we put it out," Rick said by way of a compromise. Did Jake have something to hide? Had that come out while Rick was talking on the phone?

They said their final goodbyes and Rick could see Becky was less than pleased with him. But he wasn't going to discuss that in front of the premier.

They were back in his Jeep and driving down the road before Becky turned on him. "Why won't you allow him to vet what we're going to print?"

"Because it's our interview and our magazine. I want

to make sure this interview stands out from any number of Q and A's he's done over the years." What they had wasn't outstanding, but it was still an exclusive.

"Correction, Rick. It was *my* interview. It was only thanks to me that we got it."

"But you did it under the auspices of a magazine that *I'm* in charge of. So it isn't your exclusive property, Becky. And we don't give approvals on interviews." Why did she care? Nothing earth-shattering had come out of it. At least not the part he was in on.

Becky said nothing for a few moments, and as Rick glanced at her, he caught her looking at him.

"We just finished doing an interview that you wanted to do for a number of years. You should be thrilled."

"I wished we could have sat down and gone over the direction of the interview beforehand." Becky had balked when he had asked that. "It did wander a bit."

"I know. But I got what I wanted."

"And what was that?"

"Information on his pet project. That's something that ties in with business, doesn't it?"

Rick pulled over to the side of the road, parking alongside a hay field. A farmer was cutting, the sweet smell of the grass soothing away his surprising anger.

"Why are you stopping?"

Rick turned to Becky, wishing he could sort out the confusion of his feelings right now. Yes, he had just come from one of the most sought-after interviews in his life, but it had yielded nothing. Had Becky allowed him to run the interview he would have hit harder. He had pinned so much on it and it had faltered. What they had wasn't going to give *Going West* the turnaround he had promised Terry.

But he didn't voice his feelings aloud. Nor did he take his eyes off Becky. As she held his gaze, time seemed to slow, just as it had that time at the creek in the mountains. When he had kissed her for the first time.

And in spite of the frustration he had felt. In spite of the clamor of other thoughts, he reached out and gently touched her face as if seeking to draw from her the same peace he had felt with her at that moment. Carefully running his fingers through the soft silk of her hair, sighing lightly.

"Why did you kiss me the other day?" she asked suddenly. "When I fell asleep in your office?"

Rick cupped her chin, stroking it with his thumb. "I wanted to. I couldn't resist."

"So, just attraction?"

"No." Rick fought the urge to pull her closer, to kiss her again. To do so now would smack of claiming territory, and he didn't want base emotions like jealousy to tarnish what he felt for Becky. "It was more than that. More like need. More like..." He struggled to find the right word. "More like yearning for something that would fill emptiness."

Becky drew in a sharp breath, her face now turned to his. And to Rick's utter surprise, she reached out, framed his face with her cool hands and kissed him lightly on his lips.

He didn't move, didn't breathe. His eyes drifted shut as he rested his forehead against hers.

And he caught himself praying.

Praying that God would show Himself. Praying that he would be found worthy of this wonderful, amazing woman.

Becky drew back from Rick, her heart still fluttering in the aftermath of her rash action. She didn't look up at him, unsure of what she would see in his eyes.

Why were they dancing around the edges of each other's emotions? They were both adults and should be able to talk about what was happening.

But Becky wasn't sure herself how to articulate the feelings Rick raised in her. She had fought and argued with herself. She had prayed and sought guidance from the Bible.

But each time she saw him, something pure and wonderful blossomed within her. And each time she saw him, trailing behind her initial emotions were second thoughts and insecurity.

"I thought the interview went pretty well," she said softly, trying to find a unemotional common ground that would give them both their bearings again.

Rick kept stroking her skin, his movements slower now. "Do you really want to talk about the interview right now?"

Becky glanced sidelong at him, biting her lip. "If not the interview, then what? The two of us? Where we're going?"

Rick let his hand slide down her arm. "I know one thing. I care about you, Becky. A lot."

His words sent a light shiver dancing down her spine, but it was followed by a harder thought.

Do you care enough to stay here?

Rick had made it clear from the beginning that he was only here temporarily. His sudden flight after the horse trip was like a sharp underline to that thought.

And how did she feel about him?

Becky held his eyes, as if trying to see herself through his. Trying to understand why he had kissed her, flirted with her.

Rick's eyes took on an inward look. "You're allowed to say something now," he said with a nervous laugh.

She took his hand and pressed it to her cheek, her eyes holding his. "I care about you, too, Rick." When she saw his soft, slow smile, she wanted to leave her comment there. Unadorned and simple. But she was first and foremost a child of God.

Rooted and grounded in His love.

She wanted no less from anyone she was involved in.

"But I don't know enough about you. Enough about your relationship with God. You come to church, but the only time we've talked about your faith was that moment at the creek. I don't know if you're going to be staying here, or leaving—"

Rick stopped her words with another kiss. Becky gently pressed him back, shaking her head.

"I told you before, I don't believe in casual dating. If this is going somewhere..." She stopped there, afraid to go on. She needed to know how he saw their relationship, if anyone wanted to call it that.

But at the same time she was afraid to know.

Rick turned away from her, his hands resting idly on the steering wheel, his eyes focused on the road ahead of them.

"I don't know where it's going, either," he said softly. "But I do know that I've never felt this way before." He glanced sidelong at her, a half smile teasing his lips. "And I've never talked like this before. I've never gotten this far in a relationship. Never gotten to know someone."

Relationship? Is that what he called these hit-and-miss connections?

"And do you know me?"

Even in profile his smile lit up his face. "You're easy to get to know, Becky. You're a generous and loving person."

His compliment hit the depths of her heart.

"If I am, it's because of my family. Because of the faith they've shown me."

"You're lucky that way." He angled his head toward her. "Having someone show you the way to God."

"Are you finding your way there?"

Rick's smile faded, but he kept his gaze on her. "It's hard, Becky. I've got too many questions and haven't heard a lot of answers. Either in church, or from the Bible. I haven't had the example of loving faith that you've had."

"What about your grandfather?"

As Rick pushed himself away from the wheel, she caught a glimpse of longing and pain so fleeting she thought her optimism had created it. Then his features hardened into the mask she knew all too well. He was shutting her out again.

"I think I'd like to talk about that interview now."

His voice held a harsh edge and Becky could see from the clench of his jaw, from the narrowing of his eyes, that he had retreated into a cold, hard place. He wasn't going to be telling her anything more.

Becky drew herself back against her seat, wrapping her fingers tightly around each other, disappointment sifting through her. She thought for a moment he was going to open up, show her some of his life. He held so much to himself.

How could she have let herself fall in love with a man so completely her opposite?

She let her mind linger over the word.

Love? Was that what she felt? This pain that accompanied every thought of him? The confusion she felt in his presence?

She loved the Lord, but that love nurtured and sustained her. It didn't make her want to cry.

She drew in a long, lingering breath, as if reorienting herself to his new position.

"I'll write it up, like I did with the horse pack trip," she said. "And you can look it over."

"I would prefer if we could work on it together," he said quietly. "I'd like more of a hand in shaping it rather than getting to be the critic afterward."

In spite of her swirling emotions, her confusing thoughts, she had to smile at his cryptic comment.

"As soon as we get back to the office, I have a meeting to go to," he continued. "And I'm busy tomorrow. Could I come tomorrow night to go over it with you?"

"I have a meeting at eight-thirty tomorrow night."

"I can come before."

"My family will be around, but I'm sure we can find a quiet place." In spite of her confusion, the thought of having him at her home sent a faint thrill through the disarray of her emotions.

"I'll be there at about eight o'clock, if that's okay with you?"

She almost invited him to supper, but wouldn't that smack of desperation? Better to keep things casual.

And how was she going to do that when each time

she saw him, she grew more and more attracted to him
when she knew she shouldn't?

"Welcome back, Rick. Good to see you." Dennis Ellison, Becky's brother, greeted him at the door with a
grin. "Becky's waiting for you in Dad's study."

As Rick followed Dennis through the kitchen,
warmth and the tantalizing scent of baking mingled
with coffee assailed him, followed by a sense of coming to a place of sanctuary. A place where you could
simply "be."

"Hello, Rick." Cora looked up from the tray she was
getting ready. "You came just in time. I was about to
serve up some fresh blueberry muffins."

"He can't, Mom. Becks told me to make sure I get
him to her right away." Dennis flashed Rick a wink.
"She's a bit bossy, our Becks is."

"Becky doesn't need to be such a slave driver." Cora
smiled at Rick and took him by the arm. "Dennis, you
bring the tray and meet us in the family room."

"What to do, what to do?" Dennis sighed, but did as
his mother requested.

Leanne and Colette were draped over the worn
couch. Leanne was filing her nails and Colette was talking on the phone while flipping through a magazine.

Sam lay stretched out in his recliner, his head tipped
to one side, faint snores issuing from his mouth.

"Coffee's on," Cora announced, setting the tray on
the table. "And we have company."

The girls looked up at Rick. Leanne's smile blossomed and Colette gave him a quick wave.

"Come sit over here," Leanne said, jumping up from

the couch. "Letty, get off the phone. You can talk to Nick some other time." Leanne tugged Rick's arm, leading him to the empty spot Colette made for him by pulling up her legs. "Nick is Colette's boyfriend. She's trying to decide if she should marry him or go back to school or travel. What do you think she should do?"

"I've never had to make that kind of decision before," Rick said. "So my advice isn't worth much."

Leanne sighed and pulled him down onto the couch. "I think I'd travel."

"Becks says you've done a lot of traveling," Dennis said, dropping onto the floor by his father's chair. "So you have any advice? I want to head out someplace next spring. Someplace different."

"I liked Thailand, though many parts of it are really commercialized. Bangladesh was interesting, but a very sad and hard place." He paused, trying to articulate emotions he could still feel when he thought of that country. "I've been there twice and each time I come back, I feel such a mixture of emotions. Gratitude and at the same time..."

"Guilt?" Cora put in, pouring the coffee from a carafe.

"Exactly. The gratitude I know what to do with. Never the guilt."

"The only reason I know about the guilt is we have a friend who goes to Bangladesh each year," Cora said, handing him a mug of coffee and a warm muffin on a tray. "He collects money and brings it to an orphanage there to help them purchase things they need. He says the same thing, but he does feel that what he does makes a difference. That he's helping."

"Maybe I should go with him next time," Dennis

said, stirring some sugar into his coffee. "That way I could travel and help at the same time."

"He's always asking people to come along." Cora shook Sam's shoulder lightly and set his coffee by his side. "We have company, Sam."

Sam stretched and looked around the room, his eyes vacant. Then he blinked, focused on Rick and smiled. "Welcome to our home, Rick. Good to have you here again."

And Rick felt a surge of warmth. Three times this family had so easily taken him into their home. Made him feel welcome. He wondered if Becky realized how fortunate she was.

Colette got off the phone, grinned at Rick and took a muffin off the tray. "Where's Becks? She was in such a dither after supper 'cause Rick was coming. I thought she'd be here already."

"Colette!"

"Letty."

Leanne and Cora reprimanded her simultaneously. Colette just winked at Rick. "It's the truth, ain't it? She couldn't decide what to wear, how to do her hair. I've never seen her like that."

The pleasure Colette's comment gave him surprised Rick. He couldn't imagine Becky in a dither. Especially not in what appeared to be a dither over him.

He took a sip of his coffee and as he set his mug down onto the table he looked up. And there she was. Her hair loose, just the way he liked it. A peach-colored shirt brought out the flush in her cheeks. She wore low-riding blue jeans and her feet were bare.

She looked beautiful.

"I'm sorry you got corralled into my family's coffee time." She walked over to the coffee table and toed her brother in the ribs. "I thought I asked you to bring him to Dad's office?"

"You did, dear Becks," Dennis said, catching her by the ankle. "But Mom's a bigger boss than you. And if you have a problem with that, I'll pull you down."

"Why am I not surprised? You're always pulling someone's leg," Becky said, shaking her foot loose. Dennis's groans were joined by his sisters'.

"Oh, that's nasty, Becks."

She flashed them each a saccharine smile that melted away when she met Rick's gaze.

"Have some coffee and a muffin, dear, before you get back to work," Cora said.

But Becky shook her head. "I've got too much to do." She gave Rick an apologetic smile. "Do you mind if we get at it right away?"

Rick shook his head as he picked up his mug and plate. "Can I finish this in the office? I haven't had homemade muffins for years."

"You have to take some home," Cora announced. "Becky, you make sure you package some up for him before he leaves."

Becky just nodded and, turning, led Rick down a narrow hallway to a spacious room, just off the family room. In the center of the room was a large flat-top oak desk. Bookshelves lined one wall, the other held a collage of framed pictures that covered every square inch of space above a long credenza that held more portraits.

She closed the door behind him. "Just put your stuff on the desk. I thought we could work there."

Rick did as he was told, but his eyes were on the framed photographs. Children of all ages and groups looked back at him.

"These must be of your family," he said, irresistibly drawn to the wall. He glanced them over, then pointed to one of a young girl sitting on a horse, grinning a gap-toothed smile. "I'm guessing this is you?"

"Not bad," Becky said, coming to stand beside him. "One of the other times I was on a horse. That was taken at my grandmother's new place."

Rick glanced over the mélange of pictures, his gaze snared by a couple standing self-consciously in front of a mass of flowers. "You and Trevor?"

"Grade twelve graduation."

"The cowboy and the editor."

Rick glanced back at Becky who was avoiding his gaze, now busy with a stack of papers on the desk. "I've made a word-for-word transcription of our interview with the premier. That way we can decide which angle we want to take." She was all business now and Rick took her cue, though he kept thinking about what Colette had said. Becky. In a dither.

"Do you mind if I skim through them first?" he asked, picking them up. "Did Trixie type them for you?"

"No, I did them myself. Just finished them now. They might be a bit hard to read. Dad's printer is a bit low on ink."

She leaned back on the desk while Rick took an empty chair. It didn't take him long to look it over. He had made his own notes on his part of the interview after their "chat" in the Jeep. When Becky had kissed him.

And he had kissed her back. And they had talked. And she had come so close...

Focus, Rick, focus.

A few minutes later he put the papers down and bit his lip. "You've got some good stuff here to work with. I like the gardening angle. Gives the piece a personal touch. I know that's not been done before."

"How would you know?"

Rick glanced up from the notes. "I've been covering this guy for a while, trying to get an interview. I've read just about every interview that's been archived on the Net, every report on him in every major newspaper in Canada and quite a few abroad." He looked back at the papers. "The interview isn't complete, is it?"

"What do you mean?"

"It doesn't go much past what I heard before I took the phone call from Terry at the bank."

Becky shrugged his comment aside. "We discussed personal stuff after that."

"On or off the record?"

"Off."

Rick saw the tape recorder beside the computer and pulled it over. "Can I listen?"

"I don't think that would be a good idea. It was personal."

"But it's on the tape. You were still recording it."

She nodded, edging up onto her father's desk.

"Then it's not personal." Ignoring Becky's protests, Rick hit Play and listened. He fast-forwarded the tape, but didn't have far to go. Becky had stopped transcribing shortly before the phone call. Just at the point in the interview when the atmosphere had changed.

When Jake started to talk about a girl named Kerra. He listened while Becky fidgeted restlessly in front of him.

"Kerra and I parted ways a long time ago," Jake was saying, his voice quiet. "It is the one regret that I have."

"Why do you say that?" Becky's softly modulated voice came across on the tape, and Rick remembered the way she leaned closer, her gentle features expressing a concern that made Rick himself want to confess every secret he held.

Jake hesitated, his innate caution seemingly holding him back. "She was the only woman I truly loved. She was the only one..." Another long pause.

Rick hardly dared to breathe sensing a moment of disclosure.

"I loved her but I treated her wrong. So wrong," Jake whispered finally. "I was young and ambitious. I had an advisor even then. An advisor who saw in me the potential to move higher and higher. He gave me bad advice."

Another silence. "What kind of advice, Jake?" Becky asked.

"He told me to get rid of her. And I did. And after I did, I found out she was expecting a child. And I didn't do anything about it. I left her on her own and didn't take responsibility."

Elation thrilled through Rick at his confession. This was what they were waiting for. The big breakthrough.

But as he thought about the young girl, anger chased away his jubilation.

This man had done the same thing to this Kerra girl that his own father had done to his mother. Left her a single woman trying to raise a child, dependant on family. Dependent on a cold man whose shame kept Rick at arm's length.

"Do you know where she is now?"

Rick pulled himself out of his own emotional quagmire to concentrate on Jake's reply.

"She changed her name, stopped singing and moved away. Her mother was an alcoholic and either didn't know where she was or wouldn't tell me. She died a couple of years after Kerra left town. She was my last and only link to Kerra." Jake drew in a deep breath. There was a long pause and Rick wondered if the interview was over.

"Of course you realize all this is off the record, Becky," Jake said, his voice changing back to the stern and controlled politician. "I should never, ever have told you this."

"*Going West* is not aiming to be a tabloid magazine," Becky replied.

Then a click and the tape was finished.

Rick leaned back and released his breath in a long slow exhalation. This was the scoop he'd been waiting for. This was the breakthrough that was going to make the difference he needed.

"We're going to use this, Becky," he said, tapping the papers into a neat pile and laying them carefully on the desk. "His comments. At the end of the interview. I want to use them."

"They were off the record."

"He only said that at the end." Rick glanced up at Becky, who was frowning at him, her arms folded over her chest.

"That's really splitting hairs. He told me that in confidence, Rick. While you were away, talking on the phone. And while he maybe didn't follow so-called correct procedure, this wasn't a police interview."

"No. It was an interview conducted, for the most part, in front of two people and quite publicly recorded on tape the whole time." Rick leaned forward, as if trying to force his will on his reluctant editor. "This is the article I've been waiting for. The one that will turn *Going West* around."

Becky pushed herself away from the desk, pacing around it, her head bent. "And that's all that counts, isn't it? No matter what the cost."

"It was my job when I came here. You knew that." Rick could feel her frustration pushing at him, and for a moment he hesitated. The magazine was floundering. The money was getting tight. Now more than ever he needed the boost this article would give the magazine. "You need the job, too. If this magazine fails, what will you do?"

"I'd sooner lose my job than put this out for everyone to read." Becky placed her palms down on the desk. "I'm not going to allow it, Rick. It's not right."

"He knew what he was doing when he allowed us to do the interview. It's the truth and I think we have a responsibility to print it."

"It's his own private pain. We have a responsibility to leave that alone."

"It's the truth. And sometimes truth hurts. And as for his pain..." Rick paused, fighting his rising anger. "What about the pain of the girl and the child he left all alone? He abandoned both of them. Abandoned his responsibility to them. Doesn't Kerra have any rights? Doesn't their child?"

"That's not the point."

Rick banged the flat of his hand down on the transcript of the interview with an angry slap. "It is exactly the point, Becky. He holds a public office, and what he has done directly reflects on that office." He spun around and drew his hands over his face, trying to pull his emotions together. Focus. Focus. But he couldn't keep his emotions out of this. It was too close. "He has no right, had no right, to leave that woman and that child in the lurch. Their story needs to be exposed, as well. It's the truth. And truth is part of what good reporting is all about." He sucked in a long slow breath, willing his pounding heart to slow its erratic beat. Willing the storm of his own pain to stop hurting.

"This truth will hurt and break down, Rick."

"It can also be liberating. Have you ever thought of that?" He walked slowly to the wall of pictures again.

Becky came to his side. He could feel her resistance, measure the tension in her body.

"Why does this matter so much? I've never seen you this emotionally involved in any article we've ever done."

Rick let his gaze flick over the pictures. Pictures of parents, grandparents, brothers, sisters. Posed family pictures. Candid pictures. A legacy and a heritage. How could he explain to Becky why Jake's mistake mattered so much? Becky who came from such a loving family. Would she have even an inkling of what he'd had to deal with?

He picked up a family picture. Becky flanked by her sisters and brothers, mother and father hovering over them all, grandparents on either side. His lack of family was no deep secret.

But his pain was. As was his dislike for his grandfather and the control he exerted over his life. His anger with Colson had been his constant struggle on his slow return to faith. And his anger translated into anger with God. Would Becky, sweet loving Becky, even begin to understand what emotions swirled beneath his smile?

"We need to tell the truth."

"But what is truth, Rick? It's an age-old question. Bald statement of facts that can break down and destroy? You know what this would do to his career?"

Rick turned then. "And what about what happened to Kerra? What has happened to her life? Don't you think her story should be told?"

"Not in this article."

"Then when?"

"That's not our responsibility, Rick."

And that was that. Rick withdrew, but held his ground. "This article is going to make all the difference to the magazine. We're going to run it the way I want to."

Becky drew back from him, her eyes snapping. "Doesn't matter who gets hurt, does it? As long as you can get the article that will turn this magazine around, and let you prove yourself to your grandfather."

"He's not a factor."

"I think he is. If it's truth you are so concerned about, you better look at your own reasons for using Jake this way. You're going to hide behind the so-called truth to get what you want. Just like all the other pieces you've written."

Her accusations stung and his only defense was to attack. Push her back from the truth he almost told her this afternoon. He didn't dare allow her closer.

"You sound like you're afraid of the truth," Rick

said. "I always have to push you to acknowledge that in your own work. It comes out in your other writing, as well."

"My 'other' writing is fiction, Rick. It's the truth distilled."

"But is it a truth for you? You could be a better writer if you faced the truth of your life. Your book was exactly as I described it. Sentimental and shallow. It skipped over the surface. You're a better writer than that, Becky." His words spilled out past the polite barriers he had put in place, past the diplomacy that came hard to him at the best of times.

Part of him urged him to stop, asked him why he was doing this.

Offense was the best defense. He couldn't afford to let himself get involved with anyone. Least of all someone like Becky, who was already too close.

"If we're going to talk about fear, how about discussing fear of failure? Don't you think it's easier to plunge yourself into community and church work than to make the commitment to becoming a better writer?"

"You didn't help matters any. You and that nasty book review. Also the truth, I imagine."

"Don't hide behind me," Rick said, holding up one hand. "Don't hide behind what I wrote. You've ridden on that excuse too long. You have talent and brains and ability. Too much maybe. But you make yourself indispensable to the community so that you can hide behind that, as well. If you want to be the writer you claim you want to be, you need a stronger vision. A stronger commitment. You need to say no to a few things. To realize that maybe when you do, someone else might come and take your place. And whether you like it or not, that is the truth for your life."

Becky took a step back, her voice quiet now, her face pale. What had he done with his rant? His big plan for her life.

"You talk about truth when you can't even tell people the truth about yourself." She paused. Held his gaze. "Tell me the truth now. Why does this matter so much? Why do you want to use the truth of what happened to Jake to hurt him and ruin the good he's done?"

Her questions probed, picked at threads from the fabric of his life that she had already loosened. What would it matter if he told her? What would he be giving her?

She knew how he was raised. What she didn't know were the emotions at his core. His fears. The yearnings for love that he had always disdained as weak. Needy.

But he had let her into parts of his life no one had been before. She had shown him living faith. And a pure love.

They were a potent combination that frightened him. But her gaze held his, her eyes seemed to catch his hesitation, encourage disclosure.

He retreated further.

"It matters, Becky, because this will sell magazines. And that's what we do." He looked down at the desk, unable to look her in the eye, feeling like a traitor. His own brave words about truth mocked him, but if he gave her more of himself, he would leave too much behind when it was time to go.

And he would go. He had to.

A beat of silence. Then Becky stepped back as if finally understanding what she was going to get from him.

"If you write this article, revealing the premier's secret against his will—" Becky raised her hand as if making a vow "—I'll quit." Then she turned and left through the doors leading to the yard, the sound of the door like a gunshot in the silence.

Rick slammed his fists against the desk, then ran out into the yard, calling her name.

"Leave me alone, Rick," she called out. "Go write your article."

Rick stood on the edges of the light spilling out from the open door behind him, trying to see where she was going. But she had been swallowed up by the night.

With a frustrated sigh, he spun on his heel and strode to his vehicle. He vaulted into it, twisted the key of his Jeep. As it roared to life, he glanced back at Becky's house. At the three people silhouetted against the window.

Surely Becky would enlighten them.

He reversed, slammed the gearshift into first and spun out of the Ellisons' yard. At the road he turned left, away from town, out into the dark countryside. The only sound was the throb of the engine, and the hiss of air slipping past a half-opened window. His lights cast a dim beam over the road, which swallowed up by the heavy darkness as he approached.

As he drove, her words echoed and twisted through his brain.

"You're an empty shell, Rick."

"Why does this matter so much?"

He pressed harder on the accelerator, but he couldn't outrun her words. They piled on top of each other, pulling down the barriers he had erected against her, at the same time, drawing him to a place he had been before.

And each time she brought him there, he gave her a little more of himself and allowed her closer.

And what was so bad about that?

He was leaving, that was nonnegotiable.

Why couldn't he stay? Why not?

The question spun through his head as he stared sightlessly at the road, the ditches barely illuminated by his headlights.

Put down roots? Allow people into his life?

Did he dare?

Lord, what do I do?

His cry to a God he hadn't spoken to came from the depths of his sorrow. His need.

Tell me what to do, Lord. I'm working without a net here.

Then a flash of brown. Red reflected in twin pinpoints of light facing him on the road ahead. The eyes of a deer standing in the middle of the road.

He slammed on the brakes, spun the steering wheel just as the deer jumped.

A sickening crunch. Pain that exploded through his head. His chest.

Then nothing.

Chapter Twelve

Becky's meandering feet took her back to the house, shame dogging her steps. She had struck out at Rick in anger, using words that cut and hurt, issued ultimatums she would never keep. Then, worse yet, she had run away instead of staying and facing the consequences of her actions.

"Please forgive me, Lord," she whispered, lifting her head to the night sky. *"Forgive my hard words."* She prayed that she hadn't hurt him with her truth the very way she had accused him of hurting people with his.

Rick wasn't empty. He had depth of character and a candor that didn't hide behind fancy words. His relationship with God was based on the same kind of honesty.

Now she had to find a way to apologize to him. To regain lost ground. Because in spite of words thrown out in anger, she couldn't let him go.

She slipped into the house through the doors leading into her father's study. She needed to call Rick. Find out where he was and try rebuild what she had so foolishly broken down.

As Becky dialed his number, she glanced at the notes he had left behind. The fateful interview. Yes, it still mattered, but obviously it also mattered to Rick. And in spite of how she felt about Jake's confidences, Rick had a point. Jake held a public office and as such, his private character was as much a part of that as his public one. But how could she be fair and just at the same time?

Rick's answering machine picked up. "Please pick up, Rick, if you're listening. I'm sorry I got so angry. Phone me on my cell phone. Please." She didn't care that she sounded like she was begging.

As she tried his cell phone, her heart started up. It rang six times, each ring sinking her spirits further. Then, finally, he picked up.

"Rick, this is Becky. I'm sorry. Please forgive me." Her words rushed out in her eagerness to make a connection. "I want to talk to you. I was wrong...."

"Becky?"

She stopped. The voice on the phone wasn't Rick's. Her face burned as she realized her mistake. "Sorry. Wrong number."

"No. Becky, don't hang up. This is Earl McCrae. I'm using Rick's cell phone."

"Why?" Other than the occasional chitchat at Katherine's coffee shop, Rick hardly knew Earl. What was he doing with Rick's cell phone?

"Becky. Listen to me. There's been an accident. Rick was involved. I was the first one at the accident and used his cell phone to call the ambulance."

Accident. Rick. The words caught like barbed hooks, tearing and slashing.

"Where? How? Is he okay?"

"The ambulance just left. He hit a deer with his Jeep."

She felt a sob push up her throat. Her head spun as she dropped the phone. Rick. *Lord, forgive me.*

She stumbled past the desk, heading for the door, shock numbing her movements.

"Becky. What's wrong?" her brother called out as she lurched through the family room. "I thought you had a meeting?"

"I have to get to the hospital." Becky glanced wildly around, as if looking for answers. "It's Rick. He's been in an accident."

She saw her mother half rise from her chair. Her father's shocked face. Leanne and Colette both cried out.

Dennis caught her by the shoulders just as her legs gave way. "You can't drive, Becks. I'll take you."

Seconds later they were in Dennis's car, flying through town. All she could do was pray inarticulate prayers while fear and panic lurked at the edges of her mind.

She couldn't. She had to concentrate. Rick needed her.

"You don't know how bad it is, Becks. Don't think the worst," Dennis said, downshifting as he approached a red light. He slowed, glanced left and right and gunned it through.

The hospital was just ahead and, as Dennis prepared to turn into the parking lot, she saw the flashing lights of the ambulance coming from the other direction, heard the ominous wail of the siren.

Becky grabbed the door handle, ready to jump out as soon as Dennis stopped the car. But he caught her with one hand as he spun the wheel for the turn into the parking lot with the other.

"Wait, Becks," he said. His voice was soft but his grip

brother-tough as the car rocked to a halt. "I'm coming with you."

The spinning red and blue lights kicked her heart into high gear, but she forced herself to wait for Dennis to turn off the car. Undo his seat belt. Then hers.

She jumped out, her eyes drawn to the ambulance now pulling up to the emergency entrance. Dennis caught her by the arm again, leading her along.

The back doors of the ambulance swung open, two men jumped out, whirled around and pulled out a stretcher holding a body.

"Rick," Becky called out, her knees buckling. Dennis held her up, slipped his arm around her waist. But adrenaline surged, gave her strength and she ran.

They got into the emergency entrance just as they wheeled Rick in. Blood covered Rick's forehead, matting his blond hair, streaking down the side of his head. His one eye was swollen shut. A bag hung above the stretcher, a narrow tube running from it into his arm.

Becky slapped her hand against her mouth, holding back a cry. He looked like a war victim.

He opened his eyes, turned his head and saw her with his good eye. When he reached out his hand, she ignored Dennis, pulled away and ran to Rick's side, catching his hand in hers.

"Miss, I'm sorry. You'll have to stand back." One of the paramedics caught her by the shoulders, gently drawing her away.

But Rick wouldn't let go.

"Please, let her stay," he muttered, his hands clenching Becky's with surprising strength. Then his head rolled to the side and his hand grew slack.

Panic surged through her, but the paramedic was pulling her away.

"Miss. Please. He's unconscious."

As his words sank in, she stepped back. Two nurses and a doctor converged on Rick and he was whisked away into a curtained off area.

Dennis was right behind her, his hands on her shoulders.

She turned to him, buried her face in his shoulders and all the emotions of the evening converged. She started sobbing, her shoulders shaking as sorrow and regret surged through her.

This was her fault. She had caused Rick's accident. He'd driven off in a rage. Why had she been so self-righteous?

"Becky, let's go sit down." Dennis drew her gently to the waiting area. She didn't want to go, but didn't have the strength to resist. Dennis pulled her down into a chair, his arm still around her shoulder.

Please, Lord, she prayed. *Please keep Rick safe. Please. I love him. Don't take him away from me now.*

The words went round and round her head as she clung to her brother's hand, her eyes focused on the hallway leading to the emergency ward. She could hear the faint murmur of voices, the shuffling of feet from one of the curtained-off cubicles. The occasional muffled clang of an instrument on a tray.

What was going on?

The doors of the lobby whooshed open and her parents swooped in on them.

"Oh, honey. What happened?" Her mother sat down beside her, her hand stroking Becky's shoulder.

"I don't know." She didn't look at them, her entire attention on the cubicle as if by sheer force of will she could make Rick whole. She knew Rick's life wasn't in her hands, but she couldn't stop herself.

"Is he okay?"

She forced her gaze back to her father, who had taken Dennis's seat beside her, and tears filled her eyes again. "He looked terrible, Daddy."

Her father laid his hand on her head and awkwardly stroked her hair with his rough hand. "We have good doctors and nurses here." He smiled. "And I know you've been praying. So have we. His life is in God's hands."

And what if she didn't trust that God would let her keep him?

The horrible question stopped her thoughts cold. Her mind slowed, circling the thought. It sounded like something Rick might say.

And in that moment, she understood him a little better.

Pain stabbed through the haze. Once. Then again. Coming closer together as he swam through the syrupy darkness that held him down, slowed his thoughts.

His eyelids had been glued shut. They wouldn't open. Wouldn't open. Voices swam through his mind. His mother's. Grandfather's. Becky's.

Hushed and vague shapes of people he didn't know mixed with the voices, speaking his name. Praying.

Was death this painful?

He willed his thoughts past the agony surging through his head, his chest and pulled his lids up.

The first thing he saw was a head, lying down by his

arm. He tried to speak but only a groan came out. The head lifted and he was looking at Becky's eyes, her soft smile.

He was alive.

Becky held his hand, and before the black pulled him down again, he felt her lips touch his fingers.

"How's it going, Becks?" Sam didn't glance up from his Bible, but his quiet question was a gentle reprieve for Becky.

She sat cross-legged on the living room floor, papers scattered around her in a semicircle as her fuzzy and distracted mind tried to find some thread of coherence from Jake's interview.

Her eyes were on the paper in front of her but her mind was on Rick. And each time she thought of him, she prayed for him.

She had stayed as late as she dared last night, then this morning she dragged herself out of bed to get some work done before she went to see Rick again.

The magazine needed her now more than ever, but she felt torn between the reality of the magazine's balance sheet and the needs of her own heart.

She rubbed her eyes and flashed her father a quick smile. "It's going okay, Dad." Which was a lie, but she couldn't let her father in on the secret that came out in the interview. For now it was between her, Jake, Rick. And Kerra.

She pressed her fingers against her eyes, hearing again Jake's confession, reliving her painful disillusionment. Had she known the chaos her innocent question would have generated, she would never have mentioned Kerra's name.

She pushed the papers away, unable to figure out what to write about. What to think. Life wasn't supposed to be this complicated.

"Do you want some help?" Sam closed his Bible, signaling to Becky that she now had his complete attention. Sam always spent time in the morning on his devotions, something Becky hadn't done for a while.

She didn't have time.

Becky pushed her hands through her hair, holding it away from her face as she blew out her breath in a frustrated sigh. "I dunno, Dad. I just..."

Sam leaned forward, inviting further disclosure.

Becky looked up into his deep blue eyes. Almost as blue as Rick's. She hadn't seen much of Rick's eyes the past day and a half. He slept a lot and when he was awake, his one eye was swollen shut, the other still bloodshot. It tore her heart each time she saw him weak and helpless and in pain.

"Life isn't as easy as I thought it should be," she said finally, feeling an unaccountable prick of tears at the back of her throat.

"Rick is young and strong, Becky. He'll be up and about in no time."

"And he'll be leaving."

Sam sat back in his chair, tapping his fingers together. "And that bothers you?"

Becky swallowed against the restriction of her throat. "Yes, Daddy. Too much."

"Does he know this?"

Becky just shrugged.

"Was that what you were fighting about?"

Becky pulled her legs up to her chest, bouncing her

chin lightly on her knees, and decided to let go. She had carried the burden of Jake's secret and its consequences and needed to share it with someone whom she could trust. "Jake told me something in confidence, even though the tape was still running. Something that could ruin his career. Rick heard it and wants to use it in the article. That's what we were fighting about." And that's what probably put Rick in the hospital.

"Did Jake tell you it was off the record?"

"Not until later. Which is a technicality."

"Do you want to use it?"

Becky sighed, thinking of the precarious financial position of the magazine. The article would definitely sell papers, but was that the direction they wanted to go? "I don't. But Rick says we should because Jake is a public figure holding a public office. He shouldn't have secrets."

"What's Rick's motivation for running the article?"

"It would increase the circulation of the magazine. His main purpose for everything he has done since he came here."

"Do you think that's his only reason?"

"I don't know what to think anymore where Rick is concerned." Becky looked up at her father, her emotions wavering between her growing feelings for Rick and the reality of Rick's temporary situation at the magazine.

"Have you prayed about it?"

Becky nodded.

"With Rick?"

She shook her head. They had touched upon faith issues, but she couldn't imagine ever getting close enough to Rick to pray with him.

"So maybe you should start there. Lay your needs

and Rick's before the Lord. Together. It might help clarify both your thinking." Sam got off his chair and sat down beside Becky, slipping his arm around her shoulders. "I know you care for Rick. Maybe even love him. I also know that you don't want less than a God-fearing man in your life. Maybe you need to make that clear to Rick."

Becky laid her head against her father's shoulder, much as she had when she was a little girl. "But I don't know if it matters to him what I want."

She heard Sam's chuckle deep down in his broad chest. "I think your opinion matters a lot more to him than you realize. I've seen how he looks at you. How he listens to you."

"But he's still leaving, Dad. He has told me that again and again, as if I need to know. And we're so different. He's a traveler and I like to stay in one place. He's called me sentimental and I've called him coldhearted."

"Then use your warmth to thaw him out." Sam drew back and bracketed Becky's face in his hands. "And it wouldn't be so bad if you spread your own wings a bit. Saw more of the world than Okotoks and Calgary. I think you have things you can give each other. I think you can fill parts of his life and he can fill parts of yours."

Becky bit her lip as she held her father's gaze. "But what about faith, Daddy? You always told me that I should never enter a relationship with someone who doesn't believe. Rick has so many questions about God and why there is so much sadness in the world. It's like he's angry with God."

"If he didn't have questions about God, I would be

concerned. But his questions will bring him back to the underlying faith I feel he has. His anger shows that God matters to him. I think it might be up to us to help show him the way back. Questions and anger and all." Sam smiled down at her. "I think complacent, lukewarm people are harder for God to deal with."

"And after all this happens, what if he's still going to leave?"

Sam sighed lightly and stroked Becky's cheeks with his thumbs. "Then you might have to let him go. Love him and let him go. He needs to find his own way back home."

Becky resisted that thought. Pushed it away. Could she do it?

Chapter Thirteen

The ringing of the doorbell broke into the moment and Becky drew reluctantly away from her father's side. Her father's words hurt, and she didn't know if she could face the reality of them just yet.

Her mother answered the door and Becky heard her chatting with someone.

A tall, elderly man stood on the porch. His thinning hair was swept back from wide features. Deep blue eyes held hers, and as his mouth curved up into a smile, Becky felt a tingle of recognition.

Cora turned and drew Becky to her side. "This is my daughter. Becky, this is Colson Ethier. Rick's grandfather."

"I can see a family resemblance," Colson said, reaching out to shake Becky's hand. "I'm pleased to meet you. I've heard about you."

"I'm sure," Becky said with a sharp laugh. "Let me take your coat."

"That's okay, I'm not staying long. I have a cab waiting outside. I just want to find out about my grandson before I go to the hospital."

"He's pretty banged up. He's got a few broken ribs. He's been in and out of consciousness the past twenty-four hours. He also has a badly sprained wrist and bruises. The doctor said it would be a few days before he's up and around." Becky listed off the injuries, trying to keep her own emotions in check. It had only been a day and a night since the accident. Guilt still dogged her. It was their fight that had put him in the hospital.

Her mother had come by the hospital and had practically dragged her from Rick's bedside last night. It was only the endless demands of work she couldn't pass on to anyone else that kept her away. Otherwise she'd be sitting beside Rick right now, family or no family.

"I came as soon as I could," Colson said. "Do you think he will see me?"

Becky remembered the only conversation she had heard Rick have with Colson. Rick had been uptight and snappish for a couple of days after that. She couldn't imagine what a face-to-face visit would be like.

"Of course he would," Cora said. "You're his grandfather."

"An absent one, I'm afraid." Regret edged his words, echoed by the slump of his shoulders. "Rick and I haven't always been close."

"Then this might be an opportunity to remedy that." Cora's optimism brushed away Colson's concerns.

Becky kept her uncertainties to herself. Colson looked too tired. Too weary to hear her opinions. Rick had never said anything positive about his grandfather.

"Well, I just wanted to stop by and say hello." He looked around the kitchen with a nostalgic smile. "This home has a fond place in my memories." He looked back at Becky. "Next time you see your grandmother, say hello from me."

"Why don't you stop by her place later and say hello yourself?" Becky said. "She lives in town. I can give you her address."

Colson hesitated, and Becky went to the desk in the kitchen in that moment, grabbed a sticky note and wrote Diene's phone number and address on it.

"I don't know if I'll have time, but thanks anyway. I'm only staying long enough to make arrangements to get Rick transferred to a hospital in Toronto where I can keep a better eye on him. And as soon as that happens, I'm going to be leaving."

Becky's heart plunged. Rick? Leaving?

It was as if her father's words still hung in the air, so soon did Colson's pronouncement come after them.

"Well, I'd better get going. I have a lot to arrange." Then he said goodbye and left. Becky watched him walk slowly down the walk to the waiting cab, her heart skittering.

Rick couldn't go. Not yet. *Dear Lord, not yet.*

Awareness crept over him, tingling, as he slowly rose out of the black again. The pain had dulled but it still hovered, waiting for the wrong move.

He opened his eyes. Turned his head.

Pain flashed through his head, stabbed his eye. Wrong move.

"Hey, there."

A soft, familiar voice drew his attention up. Becky stood above him, her hands resting on the bed rail, her smile hesitant.

He tried to smile back, but his lips were too dry and cracked.

"Do you want a drink?"

He nodded, and then she was slipping a bent straw between his dry lips. He sucked the moisture in and winced at even so slight a movement.

"Just sleep, Rick. You need your rest."

"No. I slept enough." He forced his eyes open. Forced himself to concentrate on her face. So pretty. "What happened?"

"You hit a deer on the highway." Becky fussed with the sheets across his chest, smoothing them down. In spite of his pain, the motions comforted him.

"My Jeep?"

"Sorry, Rick. It's totaled."

He didn't care. He chanced a movement and lifted his right hand and grasped Becky's. "Thanks for being here."

She squeezed ever so gently and covered his hand with her other one.

"How long—" He stopped as a fresh wave of pain washed over him. Becky misinterpreted his grimace and lowered his hand to his side. But he shook his head and tightened his grip on her hand. "Don't let go. Please."

"You've been in the hospital for two days now."

Shock pushed him up into awareness and pain followed, biting and sharp. "That long?" Vague snatches of memory drifted through his mind.

He remembered forcing his eyes open for seconds at a time. Seeing Becky standing beside him. Sitting. Sleeping in the chair. Her head on the bed beside him. Always there.

He moved his head again, surprised to see various bouquets of flowers lining the windowsill of his room. "Where did those come from?"

"The staff of the magazine, people from church. My family. Katherine Dubowsky. Our minister. They all came to visit you."

He frowned, then remembered other voices. People coming and going. One voice praying. The minister. "Why would they do that?"

"Because that's what people do around here." Becky walked over to a large fruit basket. "And these came from your grandfather. He was here this morning, but he said you were still out of it."

Rick just stared at the huge arrangement, wrapped up in cellophane, topped with a red bow.

"I can open it for you," Becky said.

Rick shook his head, trying to understand. "Were you here when he came?"

Becky fussed with the bow, her agitated movements making the cellophane rustle. "He stopped by the house this morning. He asked me to call him when you were lucid. But I wanted to tell you first."

Rick remembered another hospital at another time in his life. He was fifteen and getting his appendix out after a vicious attack at the boarding school. His only visitors were two friends who had skipped school to come and see him. His grandfather had been conspicuously absent.

As he took in the flowers, the cards, melancholy unfurled through his pain. "I'm surprised he bothered to take time out of his busy schedule to come."

"You're his grandson, Rick."

"That only seems to have occurred to him in the past few years." Rick couldn't keep the bitter note out of his voice. A reflection of the relationship, or lack of it, that he had with Colson Ethier.

"He seemed sad."

He caught the fleeting glimpse of sorrow in Becky's features, but then she was smiling at him. "So how does that happen?" he asked, nodding his chin at the flowers, changing the subject. "I've made enemies at the paper, enemies in the community."

"Not enemies, Rick. Just people who didn't agree with you. At first."

"And at second?"

"You've been right, as well."

"That must hurt to admit."

"You don't know how much." Becky's smile slipped past her serious expression and he felt again the pernicious tug of attraction. The edges of his mind grew fuzzy again. He fought it. Becky was here and he wanted to talk to her. To make up for something he knew was wrong between them.

"You've been here before. I remember."

"Yes, I have." Then to his surprise she gently feathered her fingers over his forehead, brushing his hair back. He sighed at her touch, his memory of the events before the accident scribbling past the sensations he felt.

"We had a fight, didn't we?"

She only nodded, biting her lip. A tear traced a slight silvery track down her cheek. "I'm sorry, Rick. I'm so sorry," she whispered.

He swallowed and closed his eyes again, his thoughts blurring. He fought it. "I shouldn't have..." He couldn't remember what he shouldn't have. Only that a sense of wrongdoing on his part poked through the vague memories of that night. "I want to make things right."

"It doesn't matter, Rick. Don't worry about it."

Disquiet gnawed at him, and he tried to lift his head. "Please tell me."

Becky laid her hand on his head. "I will. Later."

He glanced around, still feeling uneasy. Vulnerable. Two days ago he'd been walking around in charge. Now he lay immobile in a hospital bed, pain trumping thought.

Then he saw the Bible lying on his bedside and he thought of the voices he'd heard. "Can you read to me, Becky. Please? From the Bible?" He wanted to hear her voice reading the same verses he remembered his mother reading to him. "From Psalm 23."

He heard the faint rustling of pages. Becky cleared her throat and he glanced sidelong at her image, blurred by the swelling in his eye. The muted light softened her features, lit her hair with a warm glow.

"'The Lord is my shepherd, I shall not want...'" she read quietly, her voice soothing, evoking images of care and love. And as she read, a gentle peace stole over him. He reached out to her and without looking up, she took his hand.

When the Psalm was done, she set the Bible aside. Then to his surprise, she got up and brushed her lips across his forehead. "I have to go now, but I'll be back tomorrow."

"Don't cancel anything for me, Becky."

She smiled down at him. "I've canceled everything for you." And without another word, she turned and left.

* * *

"I checked with the nurse." Gladys Hemple set a plate of assorted squares on Rick's bedside table. "She said it was okay that you have these." Gladys smiled down at Rick's slightly stunned expression. "I love baking, you know. I miss my column—" she gave a light shrug "—but you know, it was time I did something else. I was thinking about that cookbook idea you gave me. I think I'm going to spend some time on that. Never had a chance to with the column and all."

"That's great. I think it could be a bestseller." Rick smiled his most beguiling smile. Becky almost laughed at the effect Rick's full-wattage grin had on Gladys, in spite of the swelling over his one eye, the bruising on the side of his face. Not that Becky was immune. It was good to see him smiling again. Good to see him sitting up in a chair.

Even though it meant that he would be ready to be moved.

No. Don't think about that. He's still here.

Gladys sighed, her hand fluttering over the region of her heart as she returned Rick's smile. "Well, then, I'd better be going. You take care, Rick. Look forward to seeing you up and about again." Gladys gave Rick another quick smile, then left.

"You gotta watch how you hand out the charm, Rick," Dennis Ellison said, pushing himself away from the windowsill. "I thought we were going to have to get the crash cart for the old girl."

"Dennis," Cora said, glancing toward the doorway, "you be quiet now. What if she heard?"

"I'm sure she's still floating down the hall," Dennis said with a laugh.

"We better get going down that hall, too." Cora pulled Becky to her side and laid a quick kiss on her cheek. "Don't stay too long, now. Colson is coming again tonight."

Chill fingers of dread feathered down Becky's spine. Was this the last time she would be seeing Rick? Was he leaving now?

She put on a smile for her mother. "I'll be along in a bit."

Cora looked over at Rick. "You take care, too, son. We're praying for you."

"Thank you for that." Rick's smile for Becky's mother held a different quality. Almost melancholy. "And thanks for coming."

"We have to," Leanne said, with a knowing look at her sister. "It's the only way we've gotten to see Becky the past few days."

"Don't stay too long." Sam echoed Cora's words, resting his hand lightly on Becky's shoulder. "You need your rest, too." He kissed her, as well, then left.

Becky stretched the kinks out of her back. She had taken some papers along in the faint hope that she could catch up on work, but between people stopping by regularly and her waiting constantly for Rick to tell her when he was going to be leaving, she got precisely nothing done.

"That was nice your parents came," Rick murmured, still smiling.

"Like you've said before, I've been blessed with a loving family."

"God has been good to you."

Surprise flitted through her at his mention of God.

But knowing that his grandfather was coming tonight spurred her to boldness. This might be the last chance she would have to talk to him about his faith.

About how she felt.

She pushed that thought aside as unworthy. She was being selfish. Rick's spiritual well-being was far more important than her feelings for him.

"Last night, you wanted me to read a Psalm to you." Becky set her papers aside. "Why?"

She heard his slow indrawn breath, but didn't look at him, afraid her own feelings would be seen clearly on her face. She had to focus. To keep herself free.

"I remember my mother reading it to me when I was a little boy. She always told me that whenever I was alone, I just needed to remember that God was always with me." He sighed. "I tried to find Him but haven't been able to. At least until lately."

Becky looked up at that. Held his steady gaze. "Why is that?"

"Because of you, Becky."

Time fell away as Becky felt suspended in the moment. She didn't want to breathe. To think. To do anything to break the wonder.

"You've shown me parts of God I didn't think I'd ever see again. Your family gave me permission to ask questions I still don't have answers for."

"You're not the first child of God to ask questions," Becky said softly. "My father told me that the Bible is a record of God looking for His people. Going after us. God is in control of this fallen world and even evil, the evil you've seen, ends up serving His purpose."

Rick's grip on her hand tightened. "I'm starting to be-

lieve that, Becky. I'm starting to see it more and more."
He twisted his head to look at her. "I've accused you of
keeping yourself too busy, but maybe God needed me
to slow down, too. Maybe he put me here to show me
that He cares in other ways."

Becky smiled and lifted his hand to her cheek.
"Many other ways, Rick," she said softly. "So go
ahead and ask your questions. I think God wants to
hear them."

"Your grandmother said the same thing. She's a neat
person."

"Do you have many memories of your own grandmother?"

"I never knew her. She died shortly after my mother
was born."

"What about your mother?"

"I have a few memories. Good ones mostly. When I
couldn't sleep, I would sneak to her room. She would
tell me stories. Sing to me. I often fell asleep in her bed."
A gentle smile curved his lips as his eyes took on a far-
away look. "She was a loving mother."

"How did she get along with your grandfather?"

Rick's smile faded away and Becky regretted asking
the question. "She tried to please him, but no matter
what she did she couldn't negate the huge mistake she
had made by showing up on his doorstep unmarried
and with a child. Grandfather never let her forget the
shame she caused him. And of course, I was a constant
reminder of that." Rick's light laugh was edged with bitterness. "So he shipped me off."

"To boarding school." Becky pulled her chair closer,
inviting further confidences.

"A very good boarding school, mind you. After all, this was Colson Ethier and he did have his standards."

"Did you see much of your grandfather?"

"On holidays. He'd give me the obligatory Christmas presents and he'd be around for Thanksgiving. But whenever I came home, he was entertaining other people. I spent more time with the housekeeper than with him."

"Why would that be?" Becky remembered the sorrow in Colson Ethier's voice when he stopped by her parents' home. This didn't fit with the picture Rick was giving her.

"I'm sure he was ashamed of me. My mother wasn't married. She never did tell him who my father was." Rick laid his head back against the chair. "He couldn't figure out how to introduce me to his friends. I could tell he was incredibly awkward, so after a while, I stopped coming home for the holidays."

Rick's quiet monotone was meant to show Becky he didn't care, but beneath his words she heard a lingering pain. Her own heart contracted, thinking of a young boy, alone at Christmas, that most family time of the year.

And suddenly she understood. "Is it because of your mother that you want to write about Jake Groot?"

Rick's jaw tensed and Becky knew she had hit upon the reason for his anger. "My mother was just like that woman that he had so casually dumped and left behind. And I'm like the child he doesn't know." Rick looked up at her, his eyes narrowed. "I'm the other side of the story, Becky. The unhappy ending. The kid without a father, left alone."

Becky's heart tore in two. "Were you very lonely?"

Rick sighed and dropped his head back, as if holding the anger up was too tiring. "At the risk of sounding maudlin, I feel like I've been lonely most of my life." Then he glanced at her and the harsh planes of his features softened, his lips parted in a gentle smile. "But I don't feel that way now."

Hope lent her heart wings and Becky gave in to an urge and cupped his face in her hand. She held his gaze, her thumb gently stroking his cheek as her heart contracted with an emotion stronger, deeper, wilder than pity. An emotion that burrowed into the depths of her soul, born of moments, thoughts, conversations.

I love him.

The words drifted up from behind and settled into her heart, bittersweet and edged with sorrow.

Rick anchored her hand with his own against his cheek. "I've wasted a lot of time in my life, Becky. Running around. Looking in all the wrong places for the wrong things. Now, I'm not so sure what I want anymore. I just know it's not what I had. The only trouble is I don't know where to start now."

Becky heard his words. His sadness. She ignored her own pain to help him. Guide him.

"You can start with the Lord. He's been the only constant in your life even if you haven't always acknowledged Him."

Rick smile was melancholy. "You really believe that?"

"God is a father who doesn't forget you. He's numbered the hairs on your head." Becky reached past him and took the Bible off his bedside stand, pleased to see pieces of paper sticking out in various places. She turned to Psalm 139 and started reading. "'O Lord, You have searched me and You know me. You know when I sit and when I rise; You perceive my thoughts from afar...'" She read on, gaining her strength and conviction from what she read. "'...If I rise on the wings of the dawn, if I settle on the far side of the sea, even there Your hand will guide me, Your right hand will hold me fast...'" She looked up to see Rick's reaction. He had laid his head down on the back of the chair, his eyes closed. When she stopped, he frowned and she continued on to the end.

"See, Rick, nothing can escape God's thoughts or concerns," she said softly, closing the Bible. "Not time or place or person."

Quiet pressed between them and Becky wisely said no more. Rick had to be convinced on his own.

"I read an interesting piece last night," Rick said finally. "Job asking God questions. Then God spoke to Job out of the whirlwind and threw a few questions of His own around. Made me realize what a puny creature I am. How unworthy I am." His laugh was a soft sound clean of his usual irony. "You've helped me back, Becky. You've given me more than I can ever tell you." Rick tried to reach up to touch her, then winced in pain. "I don't deserve you."

"Don't say that, Rick. We deserve nothing. Everything we have is a gift. I'm not better, but I am connected to a source stronger and deeper than me."

"Like a tree planted by the stream. The minister spoke on Psalm 1 the last time I was in church." He held her gaze, his own expression serious and Becky felt as if she were getting pulled into the very essence of him.

She didn't want to leave. She had other things she wanted to ask him, other things she wanted to say. But her own emotions were too uncertain. It seemed the closer they grew together, the more afraid she became. The more vulnerable she became.

Could she let him go when the time came? Would it be sooner than she thought?

A light cough behind her made her spin around. Rick's grandfather stood in the doorway, his coat folded carefully over one arm, his eyes on Rick.

She felt as if she were balancing on a precipice. She didn't want to leave Rick with his grandfather, the man who didn't appreciate his grandson. She didn't want Colson to take Rick away. Not now. Not when she felt as if things were moving in a positive direction.

Help me to let go, Lord. Help me to think of what's best for him.

"Will you come by tomorrow?" Rick asked.

Becky only nodded as a knot of sorrow thickened her throat. At the doorway, she glanced back. Rick was still looking at her.

And she sent up a quick prayer for the grandfather and the grandson.

Rick's wrist was throbbing and it hurt to breathe. He should ring for the nurse to come and help him back into bed, but pride kept him in his chair. He preferred to face his grandfather sitting rather than lying down.

Colson sat down in the chair Becky had just vacated and laid his coat on his lap, fussing with the lapels, looking anywhere but at his grandson.

"I came as soon as I heard about the accident," Colson said after clearing his throat. "You were unconscious the first time I visited."

"Becky told me you came." He angled his chin toward the fruit basket. Leanne and Colette had opened it and helped themselves at his invitation. "Thanks for the basket."

"Yes, well, it is the thought, of course. Doesn't look like you're in much shape to eat hard fruit." Colson smoothed his hand over his coat, then looked up at Rick. "How are you feeling?"

"Stiff and sore. The doc says I'll probably be out in a couple of days." Rick shifted his position, pain shot through his chest and he sucked in a quick breath through clenched teeth.

"Do you want me to ring for the nurse?"

Rick waved his offer away as he rode out the pain.

The usual awkward silence dropped between them like a chasm. Rick couldn't help but compare this visit to the one with Becky's family. Words and laughter flew around them like birds. It was never still, never quiet.

Now he could hear the swish of nurses' feet on the floors outside his room, the murmured conversation that took place at the nurses' desk, the creaky clank of a cart pushed down the hallway.

Colson cleared his throat, his fingers toying restlessly with a button on his coat. "So how is the magazine going?"

"It's going okay." Which was a lie, but he wasn't going to tell his grandfather the truth. He still had time to turn the magazine around. Time to get himself out of his grandfather's snare. He wished he had never taken Colson up on his challenge.

Even as the thought formed, he knew it wasn't true. If he hadn't come out here he wouldn't have met Becky.

"That Becky girl seems like a nice person. Are you two getting along a little better?"

"Yes, actually. We've found a way to work together."

The tension his grandfather usually generated in him slipped away at the thought of Becky. She was a strength to him—he who never thought he needed strength. She had become so much a part of him, he didn't know what he was going to do when he had to leave.

"I'm not very good at this sort of thing," Colson confessed, looking away from Rick. "Much more adept at business negotiations where the facts are laid out." He stopped, cleared his throat again. "I've not done right by you. I know that."

Rick said nothing, allowing his grandfather to navigate this new territory on his own. Truth was, Rick didn't know himself where Colson hoped to end up.

"When I heard about your accident, I knew I had to come. To talk to you."

He was quiet a moment and Rick kept silent.

"For the past few years, I've been trying to find out how to fix this," Colson said quietly. Then, to Rick's surprise, Colson laid his narrow hand on his arm and squeezed lightly. "Fix the mistakes with your mother."

"What mistakes, Grandfather?" Anger edged Rick's voice. "The only mistake my mother made was to fall in love with the wrong man. And maybe the next one was to come to you for help. You were ashamed of us."

Colson nodded and withdrew his hand. "That is the unvarnished truth. I was ashamed. At first."

"Was that why we had our own wing in the house?"

Colson stood and hung his coat over the back of the chair. "Your mother wanted it that way. And, I have to confess, I didn't argue with her. It was shame, hers and mine, that kept you there. When she died, I thought

God had punished me for what I had done to her." He shook his head. "The mistakes I spoke of were the ones I made with your mother. I had done things so wrongly."

"What do you mean?"

Colson slipped his hands in the front pockets of his suit pants, his back to Rick. "When her mother died, your grandmother, I was overcome with grief. It hurt so much and I didn't want your mother to feel the same pain. I let her do what she wanted. Let her run around. She was a wild child and after a while I didn't know how to control her." He shrugged his shoulders and shot a pained glance back over his shoulder at Rick. "When I finally realized I should do something about it, it was too late. We fought over one of her many boyfriends. She left and only contacted me when she needed money. Four years later she came back with you. She didn't know who your father was. That was why I could never find him like you had asked me to."

As he spoke, Rick felt his tender dreams of his mother shifting, being brought out into the harsh light of reality. His grandfather was not a sentimental person, indeed he was starkly proud of his honesty. He could no more lie than a raindrop could fall upward. "Why didn't you tell me this before?" he asked. "I didn't know this about my mother."

"When did we ever talk?" Colson turned to face Rick, the light over Rick's bed casting harsh shadows over his sharp features. "I only knew that you loved your mother. She changed so much after you were born. Before she died, she said she found the Lord. Which I was thankful for. I also knew that I didn't want to repeat the mistakes I had made with her. So I sent you away. I entrusted your care to professionals who knew better than I did how to take care of you."

"But you were still ashamed of me."

Colson shook his head. "At first. Yes. And in my mind the only way I knew to erase the stigma of your birth was to give you the best I could. And to try to keep myself out of your life so you wouldn't turn out like your mother had." Colson drew his hand over his face, his eyes closed. "I didn't know what to do with you, but for many years I have not been ashamed of you, Rick. Quite the contrary."

"Did you ever love me?"

Colson kept his hand in place like a shield and Rick felt a lingering, twisted pain borne of many older ones.

"I loved you to the best of my ability," Colson said finally, his voice muffled. "I was not a good father. I didn't think I deserved to be a grandfather. But yes, I loved you." He lowered his hand. "I will always love you."

And as he did, Rick caught the silvery glint of tears in his grandfather's eyes. "I'm so sorry, Rick," Colson said, making no move to erase the rivulets of moisture running down his wrinkled cheeks. "I know I did wrong by you. That's why I sent you here. Atonement. You'd been running around the world, not settling down. I couldn't give you family. Community. I knew the Ellison family would take you in. Through them I hoped you would see what a family was like. How it can work."

Rick felt his anger slide away as he thought of Becky and her family.

"So the magazine wasn't really all that important."

Colson shook his head slowly. "It was a means to an end. A challenge I knew I could give you that would keep you in one place for a while."

Rick looked over at the ledge full of flowers. Thought of the church services he had attended. The times he'd spent with Becky's family. All because of a deal struck with a man hoping for better for his grandson.

"What if it didn't work?"

Colson pulled out a snow-white handkerchief and carefully wiped his tears away. "I could only pray, Rick. Pray that God would give me a second chance to let you see how love works."

Rick thought again of Becky. Of their disagreements. Of their moments of closeness.

Of his growing feelings for her. Was that love? Did he dare think that he might have discovered that elusive emotion with her?

"Will you forgive me, Rick?" Colson asked quietly. "Forgive me for leaving you alone? And then for meddling too late in your life? For not being the grandfather I should have been?"

Rick closed his eyes as his own emotions threatened to overwhelm him. He hadn't moved from his chair, yet much had happened in the past hour. And again he thought of Becky and what they had spoken of.

How could he not forgive his grandfather when over the past few days he knew he had much to be forgiven of, as well?

So he looked up at the man he had spent so much time running away from and silently held out his hand. Colson took it and in that moment the simple, wordless gesture was enough.

Colson cleared his throat and released Rick's hand.

"I should tell you I'm making arrangements to have you moved to a Toronto hospital." Colson smoothed his hand over his coat, still avoiding his grandson's gaze. "I was wrong to push you here. To issue ultimatums. I'm not going to hold you to it now. After you've healed, you're free to do what you want with your life. I haven't done well for you in the past. It's foolish to think that I can do any more for you in the future."

Rick felt as if his grandfather was holding open a door for him that he had yearned for since he came here. A chance to leave, to go back to the life and freedom he had missed so much when he first came.

A few months ago he would have jumped at the chance.

But now?

"The magazine is having some financial trouble—"

"Do you need some help?" Colson broke in.

Rick shook his head. "I want to see this through on my own," Rick said softly, thinking of Becky. "I feel like I'm a part of something that has continuity. A past and a future."

"And when you have brought this magazine around, would you stay?"

"I just might." He looked up at his grandfather and a sudden thought came to him. "For now, though, I need you to do something for me. You set up a trust fund for me when I graduated. I have never touched it. I'd like you to do something with it now."

"Just say what and when. I can arrange it this afternoon."

"And one other thing. There's a small photo album lying beside my bed. Can you bring that here, as well?"

Chapter Fourteen

"I'll be as discreet and truthful as I can, Jake." Becky twirled the phone cord around her finger, praying Jake Groot wouldn't change his mind. It had taken over an hour of talking, convincing and praying but they had finally come to a consensus on how the article was going to be presented.

"I have to confess, talking about Kerra was the last thing on my mind when I agreed to this interview."

"God moves in mysterious ways, Jake. I think this might be an opportunity for redemption for you and Kerra." Becky toyed with the tape recorder in front of her, surprised at how events had transpired. Surprised and thankful.

"Dilton is having kittens thinking about the consequences, but it's been a good incentive for him to find Kerra before your magazine hits the stands."

"I'll pray you do, Jake."

"Thanks, Becky. Whatever happens, we'll keep it quiet until your magazine comes out. It's the least I can do for you."

"You take care, Jake. And like I said, I will be praying for you."

"You're a good person, Becky. I hope the best for you, as well."

Becky said goodbye, then hung up the phone, dragging her hands over her face. The call had drained her emotionally, but as she made a few quick notes on the paper in front of her, she knew she had done the right thing.

That Jake had done the right thing.

Becky only wished she could have done it face-to-face, but Jake's and her schedule didn't allow for it.

It had taken some time for Becky to come around to Rick's way of thinking. The truth needed to be told, but in a way that freed Jake from his secret. Told in a way that built up and encouraged and at the same time was honest in its dealing with the subject matter.

As she turned back to her computer to type in what she had written, she thought again of Rick. Of his sorrow. Of the shame his mother had had to endure, being a single parent.

She composed on the fly, images of Rick and Jake intertwining in her mind. The child of an unknown father and the father of an unknown child. It were precisely these images she'd kept in mind when she'd spoken to Jake and convinced him to let her take a different direction with the article.

Now she mined these same images, reaching for the right words, the correct phrases, the proper imagery. Her fingers flew over the keyboard as the words poured out of her. She read, corrected and reread, moving inexorably on to the end.

When she finally got there, she felt a momentary sense of disorientation.

Then she blinked, looked around her office with weary eyes and frowned at the numbers on her clock—1:15 a.m.

Her shoulders ached and her head was tired, but a sense of elation filled her. She didn't reread the piece, but instinctively knew that this was one of the rare and priceless times that she had taken an ephemeral idea and faithfully transferred it to words on paper.

Painters must feel this way when a painting they've created matches the image in their head, she thought, stretching her stiff arms above her head. She had stepped out of her own comfort zone, pushed herself into an unknown place and this article was the result.

As she lowered her arms, she caught sight of a travel brochure she had, on a whim, picked up from the travel agency. It was a typical tropical scene. Waving palm branches above an azure ocean. Tanned, fit couples lazing on the beach, doing nothing productive.

So tempting.

She had canceled a lot of meetings to spend time with Rick. To be by his side as often as possible. And it hadn't been as hard as she had thought. People had filled in. Tasks she thought could only been done by her had been completed. This afternoon, she got a call from one of the mothers of the youth choir. The minister had told the mother about Becky's "boyfriend" being in the hospital and she was volunteering to help out in the interim.

Rick was right. Saying no wasn't as hard as she thought it was. And though she still had to battle her own guilt, at the same time it had given her an exhilarating sense of freedom. It had given her empty time. Time that she could choose to fill.

Something she hadn't had in years.

She saved the file to a disk as a backup, turned off her computer and trudged out of the office to her car. She took a short detour, past the hospital on her way home, wondering what Colson had told Rick. Wondering what Rick was going to do now that his grandfather had come.

Would he change his mind about going back to Toronto? The magazine was going further and further down financially. It was looking so bad, she doubted if the article they had just done on Jake would be enough to turn the sales around.

It was out of her hands completely.

As she drove home, she sent up a quick prayer for peace for both herself and Rick.

Becky phoned the hospital the next morning to tell the nurses to notify her when Rick was going to be moved. She wanted at least to say goodbye before he left. The nurses said they hadn't heard anything about him moving just yet but that they would call her as soon as they did.

She handed in her copy and went over the layout of the issue with Cliff Anderson and his assistant. Trixie had some problems with payroll that needed straightening out and she'd had to cover for Rick on an appointment to discuss a potential advertising account with the magazine.

Each time Becky's phone rang, her heart stuttered.

She pushed and prodded and worked through her

lunch, but in spite of it all she wasn't done until eight o'clock that evening. She hadn't had time to eat and had managed on sweetened coffee all day. Her head was buzzing by the time she locked the office door behind her.

She made the trip to the hospital in record time, her palms slick with sweat. What if the nurses hadn't told the new shift that she needed to be called? What if he was gone already when she got there?

She tried to stifle the momentary panic that gripped her, but by the time she made it to the station where Rick was, her mouth was dry and dread pushed against her throat.

She pushed open the door to his room and ice slipped through her veins. His bed was neatly made up. She walked farther into the room as if to verify.

The room was empty.

He was already gone.

A sob climbed up her throat and tears welled in her eyes as she gazed wildly around the room as if seeking some hint of his presence. *No, please, Lord, not without saying goodbye?*

But the flowers still sat on the ledge. His bedside table was still cluttered with his personal effects. A book. The Bible. His photo album.

Becky swiped the tears from her eyes and picked it up. She flipped through it, surprise edged with confused excitement sweeping through her. There was page after page of different pictures.

All pictures of her.

"Hey, Becky."

She spun around at the sound of Rick's heart-stopping voice.

Colson was pushing Rick in the wheelchair into his room.

"You're still here. You didn't leave." She fell back against the bed, relief sapping the strength from her knees.

"No. I've still got a magazine to run." Rick motioned to his grandfather who nodded, smiled at Becky and left the two of them alone.

Then Rick pushed himself up from his chair and walked carefully toward her.

"Rick, be careful," she said, stretching her hand out to him, unsure of how to help him. His ribs would still be sore and his one arm was in a sling.

"I'm not going to break," he said quietly, coming to stand at her side. He looked down at the photo album in her hands. "I see you found the pictures."

Becky couldn't stop the blush that warmed her neck and cheeks as she laid it aside. "I thought it was your other album. The one with the travel pictures in it. I wanted to look through it again."

"Why?"

"I was thinking of planning a trip. Maybe going somewhere once I have some free time."

"Would you go alone?"

"I'm not a brave traveler, so I doubt it."

"If you need a guide..." Rick let the sentence hang, and Becky felt a sliver of happiness pierce her heart.

"I might take you up on that."

Rick faltered and Becky caught him by the arm. "You better sit down."

He walked to the chairs by the window and carefully lowered himself into one. "I feel a little wobbly yet. Physically anyhow."

Becky smiled and sat down beside him, trying to figure out where to take the conversation next. She wanted to ask him about the pictures. Wanted to ask him why he didn't leave.

"I was talking to Trixie this morning." Work was always safe. "About our financial situation. She said there was a large deposit made yesterday. For now we don't know where it came from, but it sure is an answer to prayer. Do you know anything about it?"

"I confess," Rick said, taking her hand in his, "I got Grandfather Colson to move some from a trust account he set up for me. A trust account I was always too proud to use because it came from him."

"But that's your future."

Rick ran his finger over the back of her hand, sending light shivers up her arm. She tried to concentrate. Couldn't.

"I decided to move it to a different future." He looked up at her and tilted a crooked smile her way. "If there is one."

Becky kept her eyes on his face, hardly daring to breathe.

"Becky, I'm sorry about the interview with Jake," he said quietly. "Sorry for pushing you into a place you didn't want to go. I was wrong to make demands. I was letting my own emotions get in the way." He laughed lightly. "I want you to write the article the way you want it written."

"Thank you," she whispered.

She captured his hand in hers, questions she hadn't dared voice before finally bubbling to the surface. "Was the magazine the only reason you didn't go back to Toronto?"

Rick shook his head, twining his fingers through hers. "The magazine was an excuse." He paused, then stood and pulled her to her feet. "You're the reason, Becky. I don't know how you feel about me, but I couldn't think about leaving you."

A soft flame kindled deep within her. "I love you," she said simply.

Rick's eyes drifted shut and his arms came around her, pulling her toward him. He winced but wouldn't let go. He buried his face in her hair, his one arm holding her, his other hand tangling in her hair. "I'm not worthy of you. But I love you, and by God's grace I will take care of you and become a person you deserve."

Becky swallowed the emotions that surged through her. "You've got it wrong, Rick," she said, carefully laying her head on his shoulder, holding him as close as she dared. "I don't deserve you."

Rick caught her head in his hands, turning her face toward his. "Don't say that. I'm the undeserving one. I'm the one who was running away from God. And now I feel like I'm in a place I want to stay a while."

He touched his lips to hers and Becky felt a gentle peace sift through her.

"But not too long."

Rick drew back, frowning. "What do you mean?"

"There's a world out there, remember. You told me you would be my guide. Don't tell me I've downsized my Day-Timer for nothing."

Rick laughed. Kissed her again. "And it sounds like you're going to be filling up mine."

"It's all about balance, isn't it?" Becky said, holding his beloved face between her hands. "You've shown me that."

"I'm glad I've shown you something." His expression became serious. "I'm glad I came here, Becky. Even though I resented what my grandfather had done in my life, God was using him. I'm so thankful for that."

Then he touched her lips with his, as if sealing his declaration.

"Has someone been going through my stuff?" Rick looked around his office, his lips curved in a half smile as he limped into the room.

"I needed to get at some papers," Becky said, walking to his desk. "And I left this here to show you."

Rick followed her, recognizing the binder that lay there.

"This is the final proof of the magazine that will be coming out. Jake's interview is in here."

Rick felt a tingle drift down his spine. He had trusted Becky with this. She had said nothing about it, given him no hint as to what it was about and he hadn't asked.

Now he would find out what she'd done with it.

He flipped through the pages, a gentle thrill of pride surging through him. It was a good-looking magazine, considering the budget restraints they had to work under.

He skimmed over the Triple Bar J article, taking a moment to appreciate the pictures. "This looks really good."

"I think so," Becky said quietly.

And then, there it was. The garden photos Rick took were pasted in a montage down one side of the article, creating a sense of energy from the pastoral pictures. "Who did this?"

"Cliff. I let him go with it."

"Nice job." Rick glanced back to the headline. Seemed innocuous enough. Then he started reading.

And as he did, he realized that the article Becky had written had become a perfect blend of the two of them. She had injected a gentle humor and emotion he never could, but at the same time he could hear his own voice woven through. And then, down toward the end of the article, he read it.

The facts of Jake's life written in the same, gently honest style. Written in a way that he knew he never could have done on his own, yet not in a way Becky would have written in the first month he had started at the magazine.

"How did you do this?" he asked, amazed at what he was reading.

Becky shrugged lightly, straightening a picture on the desk. "I tried to look at things from both points of view. When you told me what had happened to you, I tried to put myself in your place. Then I blended that in with what I knew of Jake and mixed in your voice." She slipped her hands into her pockets, rocking on the sides of her feet. "When I phoned Jake about mentioning Kerra in the article, he was understandably reluctant, but in the end seemed relieved. He trusted me with a lot. He's a good man, Rick. I wanted that to come out, as well."

"You showed that. You did an amazing job." Rick closed the binder and smiled at her. "It's a great article, Becky. You have a gift."

Becky said nothing, but the faint blush on her cheek told him more than any words could have.

He moved toward her and took her carefully into his arms. "Am I going to be sued for harassment if the publisher kisses the editor?"

"Seeing as how the publisher has a picture of the editor on his desk, I suppose I might allow it," Becky said with a light laugh, locking her hands behind his neck.

Rick grinned down at her, allowing himself a moment of pure joy. Then he kissed her.

Then Becky drew away.

"So what?" He wasn't so confident that her withdrawal didn't give him his own second thoughts about how she felt about him.

Becky twirled his hair in her fingers. "I was thinking that once *Going West* gets off the ground, financially, I might go to part-time hours. I have an idea for a book that's been germinating. Something you got me started on."

"Becky, I shouldn't have said..."

She laid her finger on his mouth. "Don't get all diplomatic on me now. You were right about my book. And a few other things."

"Such as..."

"I needed to be truer in my writing. More honest." She grinned up at him then, her eyes sparkling with mischief. "Maybe I'll take a page out of Runaround Sue's book. So something light. First person."

Rick caught her by the arms and gave her a light shake. "So who is this lady anyhow?"

"And I'd like you to help me with the book," Becky said, avoiding his question.

"I'm flattered. Now, Becky," he said injecting a warning note in his voice, "tell me who Sue is."

"Okay." She sighed and cut him a quick glance. "It's me."

"You stinker—"

She stood up on tiptoe and silenced him with a kiss. "It doesn't matter now, does it?"

Rick looked down at her and couldn't help but laugh. Which immediately sent a surge of pain through his chest.

"Oh, honey," Becky said, drawing back, her hands fluttering over his face, his shirt. "Are you okay?"

"I've been better," he said with a smile. "And I'm getting better all the time. Especially now that I know your deepest secrets."

"Well, that will take longer than a few days to sort those out."

"You have more?"

Becky bracketed his face with her hands. "All kinds. Like a yearning to do some traveling. To spread my wings a little."

Rick shook his head. "I can see that life with you is going to be a series of surprises."

"'...love...an ever fixed mark that looks on tempests and is never shaken,'" Becky quoted softly.

"I like that. Who said that?"

"Shakespeare, in one of his sonnets."

"And my future wife is also an intellectual."

Becky laughed. "You make me feel like I can be better than I am."

"I don't know. I love you just the way you are. But I'm hoping we can grow together. That our partnership will be rooted and grounded in God's love."

"I hope so, too," she said, laying her head on his shoulder.

Epilogue

~~🍂~~

"I want to propose a toast to the bride and groom." A man's voice rang above the din of voices echoing through the orchard. "Would someone please find Rick and Becky?"

"I guess that's us," Rick said, pulling Becky to him in a quick hug.

"We could stay here." Becky settled back against a large tree branch, shaking loose a light shower of apple blossoms. She had shed her veil shortly after their wedding pictures were taken, but kept the wreath of flowers pinned in her hair. She looked like a woodland nymph in her flowing white dress, the diffused sunlight glinting in her hair.

"Sounds tempting," Rick said, shifting his weight. "You sure these branches will hold us up?"

"For a while anyhow, though I imagine sooner or later we'll have to make an appearance." Becky brushed a stray petal off his shoulder. "Just make sure you don't rip that tux climbing down."

Rick smiled at her and was about to give her another kiss.

Then he heard light footsteps below and a face came into view through the branches. "Aha. There you are." Leanne shook one of the branches, showering them both with apple blossoms. "I figured you'd be here."

Rick looked at Becky and shrugged. "Guess not such a good hiding place after all."

Rick kissed her anyway. Just because he could. Then he helped his new wife out of the tree.

"I can't believe you went climbing in that dress," Leanne chided, fluffing out the wispy silk, fussily brushing the petals out of her sister's hair.

"Leave those," Rick said, stopping his sister-in-law. "I like how that looks."

"Such a romantic." Leanne gave them both a light push in the direction of the yard. "Now, you handsome couple, get moving. Dennis has been working on this toast for days."

Becky slipped her arm around Rick and together they walked through the orchard to the opening where their families and friends had gathered for the reception.

"There they are."

"Where were you?"

"Hiding on your own wedding."

While Cora fussed with Becky's dress, Rick looked around at the gathering. Colette caught his eye and winked at him. Sam raised a glass in their direction. His grandfather sat to one side listening to Diene who had pulled up a chair beside him. They were both smiling, as if pleased to renew an old acquaintance with a hint of more to come.

They were surrounded by family and friends, all gathered in this orchard to wish them well. To celebrate with them. Rick's heart filled with love and gratitude. If he lived to be a hundred, he didn't know if it was long enough to express his thankfulness to God for what he had received when he had reluctantly come to this place.

Becky slipped her arm around his waist. "Hey, you're looking mighty serious."

He looked down at his wife and once again marveled at her love for him. His love for her. "I'm just thankful, is all. Thankful for the paths my life took that finally brought me here."

"It was a roundabout trip if you include Malta and Thailand."

"And all the other places between." He dropped a kiss on her forehead. "But here I am and here I stay."

"I love you, Rick Ethier."

"And I love you, Becky Ethier."

"Okay, enough mooning. I have to present this toast," Dennis called out. He cleared his throat and raised a shaky glass in their direction. "Rick. Becky. This is my toast to you. May the arguments be short and the reconciliations long. May your happiness be many and your sorrows few. May your roots go deep and your branches reach out far. May your hands be empty and your hearts full. And may all the paths you take, always lead you home. To God's refuge for your hearts."

"Amen to that," Rick whispered.

Then, in the shade of trees planted before they were born, Rick took Becky, his wife, into his arms and held her close.

Close to his heart.

* * * * *

Dear Reader,

I get angry quick. I laugh quick. I talk too much and I cry easily. My husband is quiet. Thinks before he speaks. He was usually the parent the teachers liked to talk to when there was a problem with the kids. I know God brought Richard into my life because I needed the balance he gives me. But Richard has always told me that I have given him a balance, as well.

In Rick and Becky's story, Becky was grounded, rooted in her family and community, which was a strength. Rick was practical and had seen much of the world, which was also a strength. I wanted to show two people who need something from each other. Two people who'd learn to give from their strengths and accept from their weaknesses. The same thing happens in family. In community. The body has many members, and we all need to use our gifts to help each other and build each other up in Christ.

Thanks for spending time with Rick and Becky. I pray God may bless you and that you see the gifts He has given you, as well.

I love to hear from my readers. You can write to me at Carolyne Aarsen, Box 114, Neerlandia, Alberta T0G 1R0. Or you can send an e-mail to caarsen@telusplanet.net. Please put "A Heart's Refuge" in the subject line, so I know it's a fan letter and not spam.

Carolyne Aarsen

Love Inspired®

A NEW LIFE

BY

DANA CORBIT

Her matchmaking friends thought single mom Tricia Williams needed someone, and the blind dates began. No one could compare with her lost love—until she met Brett Lancaster, the handsome new man in town. But their budding relationship grew strained when Tricia learned he was a state trooper. She'd already lost one man to a risky job. She didn't know if she could put her trust in God once again and find the strength to begin a new life…with Brett.

Don't miss

A NEW LIFE

On sale October 2004

Available at your favorite retail outlet.

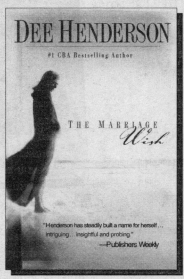

| P.O. Box 1867 | Fort Erie, Ontario |
| Buffalo, NY 14240-1867 | L2A 5X3 |

YES! Please send me 2 free Love Inspired® novels and my free surprise gift. After receiving them, if I don't wish to receive anymore, I can return the shipping statement marked cancel. If I don't cancel, I will receive 4 brand-new novels every month, before they're available in stores! Bill me at the low price of $4.24 each in the U.S. and $4.74 each in Canada, plus 25¢ shipping and handling and applicable sales tax, if any*. That's the complete price and a savings of over 10% off the cover prices—quite a bargain! I understand that accepting the books and gift places me under no obligation ever to buy any books. I can always return a shipment and cancel at any time. Even if I never buy another book from Steeple Hill, the 2 free books and the surprise gift are mine to keep forever.

113 IDN DZ9M
313 IDN DZ9N

Name _____ (PLEASE PRINT)

Address _____ Apt. No.

City _____ State/Prov. _____ Zip/Postal Code

Not valid to current Love Inspired® subscribers.

Want to try two free books from another series?
Call 1-800-873-8635 or visit www.morefreebooks.com.

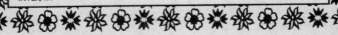

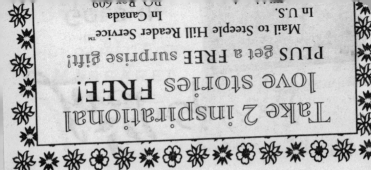
Yet it was a beautiful woman trying to save her family's horses that took his breath away. Darcy O'Brien and her young son needed a chance to start over, but neither Joshua nor Darcy was ready for a relationship, as their respective pasts had left them wary. But when the arsonist struck close to home, would Joshua risk everything for the woman he loved?

Don't miss

GOLD IN THE FIRE
On sale October 2004
Available at your favorite retail outlet.